The Alchemist's Bride

by

Evelyn Klebert

For Vivian,
as
A Love Letter
to
Her Birthplace

Table of Contents

The Alchemist's Bride

Chapter 1

The Letter

There were things about Emmeline Lescale that no one would ever know. These were things she kept hidden in a secret vault deep within her mind. Now she was not one to delude herself. It certainly wasn't knowledge anyone else in particular would consider of value or even a passing interest. But there were things that she purposefully kept private because society dictated she appear a certain way on the outside — placid, not overly conspicuous given the unsteady state of her affairs, not overly intelligent, but generally capable.

This was the role that she played on the outside. Every bit of it was a facade that she had adopted fairly early on, living off the goodwill of her aunt and late uncle, who had taken her in at a young age. These events occurred sometime after her mother had died, and her father conspicuously showed no interest in her. As it was, these were only a few of the misfortunes that had shaped the person she'd become.

Aunt Adeleine lived up the Mississippi River in a fine, old estate in Vacherie and had been more than benevolent in treating Emmeline as one of her girls, well, nearly one of them. All of the La Maire girls, three to be exact, had married exceedingly well. And Emmeline, well, Emmeline had not married and instead somewhat dutifully had remained with her aunt, and her cousin Jeanne Marie, the eldest daughter, and her husband Bernard Aldige, to be of what help she could in managing the property. That was unofficial, of course. Officially, she was preparing for some sort of career as a governess whenever the time was right.

That particular time, however, never did seem to be quite right.

During the course of her time in her aunt's household, there had actually been a few random offers of marriage, one from a local constable and another from a businessman who lived in a nearby parish. Both the gentlemen were much older than she, and her aunt had actively discouraged the matches. And the truth was that this suited Emmeline very well. This was one of those secret, hidden things about her. She didn't want to marry, not at all. The year was 1883, and women who married simply lost most of their independence, what little it was that they possessed. In her estimation, widows seemed the only genuinely independent females who could affect their own destinies. And, of course, if Emmeline could find a way to bypass the married state and move straight into the role of a widow, well. But unfortunately, that would involve the cumbersome matter of dispatching a husband with all its moral ambiguities, not to mention criminal culpabilities.

Emmeline, she indulgently liked to think, was at heart a kind person but undeniably also a restless one. She was far too intelligent to be a placid woman or to be caught up in a repressive union. So, with little resistance, she allowed her Aunt Adeleine to squash the few prospects she'd had. After all, maybe one day she would be a governess to the children of the La Maire girls. Perhaps that wouldn't be so dreadful an existence. And rather gratefully, or so she attempted to be, she'd settled into her predictable existence in the Vacherie estate, Belle Coeur, as the locals called it — *Beautiful Heart,* because all the homes with any acreage must have some kind of significant designation.

As it was, all seemed relatively fixed in terms of Emmeline's future and destiny, and she struggled with diligence to suppress her restless nature and accept that reality until, of course, it wasn't. When she had just crossed the threshold of her twenty-fifth year, then everything rather abruptly changed.

"Oh, my dear!" How she did recall that day.

Aunt Adeleine's face was blanched, even more so than it usually was, a pale, drained, sickly-looking color. She'd summoned Emmeline into the west parlor, where her aunt would spend the dawn hours answering and, most often, creating correspondence as well as leisurely sipping her morning tea.

"My goodness, Aunt Adeleine, what's happened?" There was no denying it. The older woman looked positively stricken, possibly ill in some respect, she suspected. "Do you need a surgeon, Aunt?"

She shook her head a tad bit frantically. "No, no, my dear, but you must sit. Something has transpired, and I'm afraid it will be a bit of a shock."

She struggled to appear comforting. Emmeline wasn't fond of surprises, and she was already feeling an uncomfortable cold, foreboding spot in the pit of her stomach. She settled in the small pink velvet slipper chair on the other side of her aunt's rosewood morning desk. There was a sudden chill charging up through her. Undeniably, she was extra sensitive in this regard, having a precognitive sense of impending trouble. She'd always felt it was a defensive scar left over from childhood, never quite feeling secure and solid wherever she might be.

"My dear," again her aunt repeated as she sniffled a bit, certainly appearing on the surface to be quite overwrought. "I have received a letter from your father." Aunt Adeleine was well into her fifties, and the signs of aging already marked her delicate, French aristocratic features. But framed by her still primarily black, although somewhat streaked with gray, hair were her eyes — enormous dark brown eyes that Emmeline felt, at the moment, might just pop right out of her tiny head.

"What did it say?" Emmeline asked quietly. Now, this was annoying and perplexing. Her father never wrote, never. Never to check up on her, never had in all the days she could remember, instead just seemed content to pretend that there had indeed been no child produced in his brief marriage with her mother.

"Well, my dear, shocking as it may seem at the moment, Nathaniel wants you back."

Emmeline sank down further into the less-than-comfortable velvet chair. Aunt Adeleine had seldom used the name, Nathaniel. In fact, in retrospect, Emmeline actually couldn't recall her ever using it in reference to her father. Instead, it had always been more often than not, Mr. Lescale, and occasionally, *that man*. She didn't seem even inclined to give him the privileged title of Doctor, although that was, curiously enough, how he and her mother had met.

From what she'd been told, the Charbonnet family had once owned a quite stylish residence in New Orleans' French Quarter, and Lizette Marie, her mother, while there, was stricken with a rather dire and abrupt case of scarlet fever. A surgeon was summoned, the well-respected Dr. Lescale, and from there, the liaison had taken root. Naturally, according to Aunt Adeleine, the match was frowned upon by the family, and subsequently, a scandalous elopement took place, and so on.

This was the rather flimsy story as she recalled, and beyond that, there were sparse references that her aunt would make concerning Emmeline's father, which always seemed to be followed up with *"Doctor indeed, he couldn't even manage to save his own wife."* But, of course, Emmeline had gleaned from a young age that in the year following her birth, Lissette Marie Charbonnet, or rather Lissette Marie Lescale as it was, had been stricken with a rather chronic and quick-moving case of consumption. *"What a beast not to move the poor girl out of the city and back into a more rural climate."* With that reference, Emmeline assumed Aunt Adeleine was referring to their childhood home of Belle Coeur in Vacherie, where they now resided. *"But you know Lescale was always a selfish man. Certainly, he took no interest in you, my dear, his own daughter.*"

Emmeline really had no idea how she truly felt about the subject. She had never known Dr. Nathaniel Lescale, nor had she ever known the beautiful Lissette Marie Charbonnet, who had married the celebrated physician, moving to a sprawling French Quarter mansion, then tragically dying, leaving her young child when she was only one. Of course, there was the portrait in the upstairs gallery, painted a year before she'd left. Nineteen was her age when she'd married Lescale. Emmeline was twenty-five and had already outlived her mother by several years. She looked at her aunt's pale, stricken face and wondered with distraction what nonsense this was that she was sputtering.

"What does that mean, Aunt, that he wants me back?"

Her spindly aunt pressed her hand to the ruffles on her forest green satin bodice to accentuate dramatic distress. "He writes that he is experiencing some medical complications and desires that you come to live with him to help manage the house."

Emmeline felt a quick dart of fury streak through her head, but she suppressed it, as was her manner. "What does that mean? He wants me to be his maid?"

"No, no, my dear, I'm sure he wants you to help oversee things. Although it is my understanding that he does not live in so grand a house as he once occupied when he and Lissette were first married. That is part of the reason he allowed the family to raise you, my dear."

As much as she tried to control it, her heart was thumping wildly. Surely, this would not be. This man, this stranger, would not ignore her for the balance of her life and then demand her services when he had need of her. "Aunt, is there nothing to be done?"

She nodded emphatically, fanning herself wildly with a piece of stationery she'd picked up from her well-stocked desk. "Oh yes, my dear, we will consult Charles. I am certain he will help us find a way around this business."

Chapter 2

The Journey

Charles Dufour was a solicitor, the son-in-law of Aunt Adeleine, having recently married her youngest daughter, Pauline. Already, he was ascending the ladder of success in his family's law firm in the parish of Plaquemine, not so very far from Belle Coeur.

Rather stout in stature and dark-haired, Charles was a small man. And in truth, Emmeline found him wanting. He had an air of self-importance that made her skin prickle with irritation whenever she was in his company.

"So, what do you say, Charles? Surely, we can avoid this calamity?"

Her Aunt Adeleine's voice had risen to that strident, panicked pitch that Emmeline was more than familiar with. It was the same exact tone she used when her tea was too weak, her correspondence was not dispatched on time, or when Pauline's ball gown was not fitted to perfection. All these vexations seemed to fall into that similar category of catastrophe.

Of course, Emmeline would have liked to believe that her aunt truly loved her and that she would be heartbroken at Emmeline's absence from Belle Coeur. But her realistic mind told her instead that her aunt would be highly inconvenienced by her departure, as Emmeline had managed to make herself somewhat indispensable in the older lady's existence.

"Well, hmm," Charles grumbled by the west parlor's long window, carefully perusing Dr. Lescale's letter. "It is a difficult matter. And there were no papers signed, no formal legal papers concerning Emmie's custody." Emmie was one of her nicknames in the house. With her aunt, it was always Emmeline. With Pauline and, subsequently, Charles, it was Emmie, and more often than not, it was simply Em.

"Well," her aunt began tentatively, "not really, you see, the family just took the child after Lissette died."

"So, Dr. Lescale asked you to take her?"

Another hesitation, as though Aunt Adeleine were selecting her words with great care. "Well, not precisely, my father, he arranged it," she explained haltingly.

"Arranged it?" Charles prodded gruffly.

"Yes, he went to the city and spoke to Nathaniel, and convinced him that Emmeline would be better off with us."

"And then Lescale abandoned her, didn't try to see her."

Again, there was a pause that caused her to eye her aunt critically, "Well, he tried, I understand, at first, but it was discouraged."

Charles was actively frowning at her aunt now, "Was there correspondence?" He asked more than a bit impatiently.

Her aunt stared at Charles with those small brown eyes so wide, undeniably looking quite uncomfortable, never once glancing to meet Emmeline's steady gaze. "Well, yes, there was."

"He wrote?" The words flew out of Emmeline's mouth entirely uncensored, quite unexpectedly even for her, an involuntary reflex that she was incapable of controlling.

Her aunt looked at her, her mouth oddly pinched, clearly in surprise. "Why yes, he did write."

Now, this was something she'd never suspected. "Why did I never see such letters?"

"Well," she replied sheepishly, "we thought it was best. They were read, of course, as was this one."

Charles cleared his throat intrusively from across the room. "And where are these letters, Adeleine?"

Her aunt bristled. Clearly, she didn't like him using her given name so cavalierly. "My father at the time thought it best they be destroyed."

Emmeline felt the pit of coldness that she had been living with since the matter of her father's letter was first broached deepen and expand somewhat. She wondered for a fleeting, insubstantial moment if that would have changed things, having this little scrap of contact with Nathaniel Lescale, one that was arbitrarily denied her. But then just as quickly as it had arrived, she dismissed the thought as an indulgence, as it was her cultivated nature to be a realist.

"And before this one, when was the last correspondence received?"

"Oh," her aunt began, her voice a bit shakier now. "Perhaps a month ago."

There was silence in the room except for the sound of Charles Dufour sighing with exaggeration. "Well, well, that is unfortunate," he grumbled with irritation. "A clear case of abandonment will not hold up in court, and until Emmeline is married, she is under the guardianship of her father. I don't suppose she has any prospects of marriage."

Marriage, the word hung there suspended in the room like a condemned man hanging in the gallows. "No," Emmeline responded rather icily. "I do not."

✿

Charles Dufour and his wife, her young cousin Pauline, were her escorts the following month. At first, the matter seemed to be left unresolved, more so completely unspoken of, but Emmeline could readily read the signs. More letters from Nathaniel Lescale arrived. Some, she was privy to pieces of, and some she was not. It seemed there was a case to be made for her remaining in Vacherie, but other means, unspoken, secret pressures were being applied that made Aunt Adeleine rethink her position. What was undeniable was that, on the whole, the plantation, Belle Coeur, was in a decline. Incrementally, after the War and following her uncle's untimely death, pieces of property were sold off, and workers were let go, just a small bit at a time. It was a secret, not well kept, that the once somewhat lavish lifestyle of the La Maire ladies was slowly being scaled back. And this reality, more than any other, Emmeline felt acutely, was at the heart of her departure from Belle Coeur. Given their increasing financial distress, Emmeline was not an asset her relatives felt was worth fighting for. Certainly, her aunt didn't desire to be dragged into some scandalous court battle. After all, with her dear husband Henry deceased, she was only a woman and too old for such anxieties. At least, that was the position that Emmeline construed Aunt Adeleine was taking, given her wealth of experience concerning Adeleine La Maire's character.

It would be reasonably expected, or so Emmeline thought, to perhaps have felt the pain of some kind at this betrayal. But as it was, she didn't really. She prided herself on being too much of a pragmatist for such emotions. Since she was a small child, she had felt that her tenure with her deceased mother's relatives was somewhat delicate, unstable, and thus unreliable.

The sad truth was that she had never really made a home with them. Deliberately, she had closed herself off, perhaps protectively, not allowing her emotions to connect fully with the place or, really, the people in any permanent fashion. Emmeline had always been a visitor, never letting her heart or mind forget it.

"I can't believe Mama is truly letting you leave."

Pauline, the youngest and most fair-minded of the La Maire girls, was delicate and nowhere near as demanding or obtuse as Aunt Adeleine. Out of the three sisters, she had always found her the most amiable. She was a bit smaller in stature than Emmeline, with long chestnut-colored hair and her own very wide brown eyes, not unlike her mother.

She and Charles had taken Emmeline and the trunk filled with her belongings to the dock at Vacherie. From there, she would take the steamboat down the Mississippi River into the city of New Orleans, where, allegedly, Nathaniel Lescale, her father, would collect her. It was a chilly night, one of the last days in October. She reassuringly patted one of Pauline's small, gloved hands. What could she say to her? Married or not, Pauline was still such a child.

"It's no matter, little one, just a new adventure for me." Her tone was light and carefree. No reason to further agitate her closest ally in the La Maire household.

Regardless, the frightened eyes only widened further. "But how can you leave your home, your loved ones, Emmie?"

She drew a deep, restraining breath. Her home? Her loved ones? Truly, her young cousin didn't understand anything. But then, in that delicate moment, Charles interrupted them brusquely with her boarding papers in hand. "Your things are being taken onto the ship, Emmie."

In a sudden, final, dramatic gesture, Pauline threw her arms around her in a tight embrace. "Please write Emmie, and Charles and I will come to visit as soon as we can. Won't we, Charles?"

"Well, of course, my dear." Emmeline detected the slightest mark of displeasure on his puddy-like features at the comment. She wouldn't be anticipating that particular visit any time soon.

"Don't be anxious, Pauline," she reassured. "It all will turn out well." This she said with as much cheer as she could manage, truly as much for herself as for her cousin.

✣

There seemed to be a fog surrounding everything as the Natchez steamboat traveled leisurely down the Mississippi River. There was a warm, comfortable room inside the ship where passengers conversed and partook of hot beverages. No doubt, it was more pleasant than out here on the deck. But Emmeline didn't feel in the least sociable and preferred to wait outside. She was in a curious state, somewhat removed, numb perhaps — as if not only her skin beneath her dark muslin dress had been affected by the chilled dampness of the air.

It was true that she had not taken much time in her twenty-five years of life to truly examine her heart. A case could be made that she'd actively avoided it. Instead, she had cultivated a distance, detachment within and without, a sort of cocoon of insulation. But in this peculiar moment, beneath a dark, cloudy sky of mystery and stillness, Emmeline did ask herself quietly.

What did she really want?

What a daunting question, as there might actually be options now opening for her. Options rather than people around her incessantly saying that there were none, verbally, but more often with no words, instead in their actions. Perhaps now there might be more than the expected inferences of *"Take what you deserve,"* or *"Take what you can get,"* and even more definitively, *"Take what's left for you."*

It was a curiosity, this numbness — not actually pain at the considerations but rather a distant, removed sort of reflection.

Choices were at hand now, possibilities. Just because her father had sent for her, she didn't need to do his bidding. She could take another course, perhaps melt into the city and find employment somewhere, although she was dubious as to what kind she could achieve.

Without question, she was well-read and well-educated by instructors hired to tutor the La Maire girls. She had always had a thirst for knowledge, devouring volumes in her uncle's library while her cousins were enmeshed in their schooling on how to be a lady of the manor. Well, Emmeline had never expected to be a lady of any manor, so she'd focused her mind on other areas. She was more than qualified to be a governess, or perhaps a teacher at some private girl's school, or perhaps she could work in a shop somewhere. There were real possibilities and not just the horror stories of young women forced to sell themselves on the streets in a foreboding, unknown city. Of course, these were fears her Aunt Adeleine had worked diligently to place in her mind over the years. And in retrospect, given the recent turn of events, she imagined her aunt had always been working against any latent inclination that she might have to pursue a relationship with her father.

"Well, he will not support you, my dear. I understand that he has fallen on difficult times, had to entirely give up the house he had bought for my dear sister Lissette when they were first married." These had been Aunt Adeleine's words, but now Emmeline's heart felt curiously untouched at the realization of how very little her aunt had fought for her once her father had decided that he had need of her.

Her eyes took in the calm black water of the river as the steamboat traveled on through the quiet evening. Perhaps, it was her surroundings, perhaps her upbringing, but the numbness persisted. She neither looked forward to anything nor did not. With very little mustering of emotion, she wondered how much of an inconvenience to everyone it would be if she simply threw herself into these dark placid waters. Would they receive her with empathy for the lost soul that she was or with the indifference that seemed to be the hallmark of her existence? It was a question that seemed, in this particular moment, would remain unanswered.

By the time the steamboat docked at its designated port, Emmeline had scarcely spoken a word to any of the passengers aboard, so heavily was she caught up in this day's blanket of recollections that had enveloped her. Dismally, she wondered if she was experiencing some sort of psychological depression of sorts. Of course, Aunt Adeleine had consistently feigned such maladies, always having a healthy supply of laudanum at her bedside table for such occasions.

But then again, Emmeline had always prided herself on having a pragmatic mind. One who was a realist couldn't possibly entertain any depression. A realist had no unrealistic expectations and no disappointments. Life was simply what it was — no more expected, no less.

Though still feeling markedly out of sorts, Emmeline dallied behind the disembarking passengers. Pulling her woolen dark blue shawl more tightly around her neck, it was acknowledged that she should have worn her coat instead of packing it in her trunk. It was only seven in the evening, but night had descended fully on the city. In her preparations, she hadn't considered that winter was approaching. Odd, the truly altered mindset she seemed to be in. She, who considered everything, had not considered that her first steps into a new life would take place beneath the cover of darkness.

Then again, it was not wholly dark. She noted as she stepped onto the exit ramp.

Chapter 3

Dr. Fallon

Even before she took her first steps onto the long wooden platform exiting the Natchez steamboat, Emmeline could see well past the docks to the brick buildings lining the city street. Much of the area was illuminated by lamps, in fact, so very many streetlamps. In Vacherie, the grounds of Belle Coeur with the exception of some scattered oil lamps, would be in total blackness at this time of the evening, the dense shadows encroaching on everything. But here in New Orleans, clearly, night afforded more activity than she'd expected.

When she finally finished meandering behind the flow of passengers off the ramp, Emmeline realized she had no idea who she was looking for. Everything, her departure, the trip down the river on the steamboat, had such an unreal quality that she was only now truly absorbing the reality of her situation. Perhaps she would not melt into the shadows of the city just yet to pursue her own vocation, not yet until she had a firmer grasp of what her life might become here.

She glanced about dubiously, wondering if, indeed, anyone would be meeting her. Everyone around her wore a coat, a coat, and a hat. And she only had her long shawl — not very warm and no hat — over her dark gray muslin dress.

Her wardrobe had not been well thought-out. The cold air was seeping into her skin. Deep down, she surely would never admit that perhaps upset over the recent events had led her to be neglectful of planning. That would be an unsettling admission that she'd lost control over herself, over her own emotions. And on the heels of this, accompanying the chilly weather was the realization that she genuinely had no idea how long she would be waiting.

There were quite a number of people milling about as she shivered. Emmeline wasn't used to so many in the same place at once. It struck her oddly, or perhaps for the first time, how isolated and remote her existence had indeed been. Glancing back at the boat, she noted they were beginning to unload the luggage, placing the traveling trunks and suitcases on a horse-drawn cart that would be rolled down the ramp. Fortunately, Pauline had suggested they tie a bright red satin ribbon on the handle of her trunk. Otherwise, it might just vanish in the growing heap of other similar baggage.

She turned her eyes back toward the city. There were carriages in the streets — all sorts: curricles, phaetons, victorias, broughams, and simple wagons — some grandiose, some quite akin to just an open cart.

Again, it all felt so foreign, all of it, as though a part of some strange, disconnected dream. She had never been to a city of this size before. But here she was, in 1883 New Orleans, a great yawning precipice, and she accepted, though surely not whole-heartedly, that she was not indifferent, not removed at all. And yes, undeniably, she was not really numb. In fact, in stark contrast, she was quite overwhelmed. Quite clearly, she must admit, at least to some corner of her soul, that it all somewhat terrified her.

"Miss Lescale."

Somewhat humiliating, she had almost physically jumped from being so lost in thought and startled at someone using her name. Her heart pounded wildly as she saw a man standing just next to her, whom she had not even noticed had approached.

"Yes," murmuring in a voice that could only qualify as a loud, breathy whisper.

The man beside her was tall and wore a heavy dark coat and hat — entirely sensible.

"Your father, Dr. Lescale, sent me to collect you." He held out a gloved hand, presumably for her to shake — gloves, also decidedly sensible. "I am James Fallon."

Looking up more directly, she could see his face clearly. At least as clearly as she could, given her eyesight was a bit blurry from the night air. James Fallon, she assessed, was bearded, sort of blonde, skin tone that she might describe as somewhere directly situated between tanned and pale.

Briefly shaking the hand that was offered, "Pleasure to meet you," she mumbled, still feeling awkwardly embarrassed, well, for a variety of things.

"I have a carriage," he motioned toward the street. "If you'll point it out to me, I'll have someone collect your luggage." And then he eyed her oddly for a moment and rather abruptly pulled off his long, dark overcoat, beneath which was an equally dark suit. Without a word, he dropped it over her shoulders. "It's been increasingly cold this evening. Shall we?" he gestured to the wagon in the distance, filled with luggage.

Emmeline did not reply because she was surprised at the unexpected gesture. She should have thanked him, and didn't really understand why she hadn't, except that she was profoundly out of sorts. So instead, she just began to move forward through the cold night air.

✤

Jack Fallon found Emmeline Lescale to be somewhat tall for a lady, at least tall for the ladies of his acquaintance, perhaps approaching five and a half feet, he surmised. She had a rather abundant head of thick blonde hair and eyes whose shade bordered somewhere in that inscrutable valley between brown and green. Outside of their distinctive color, he found them guarded and pensive, not something entirely unexpected given her peculiar circumstances.

His good friend Nathaniel had intended to send his manservant Benjamin to collect Miss Lescale. Of course, on hearing this, Jack interceded. It would be such an impersonal homecoming to be greeted only by a servant upon arriving at a new home. Nathaniel Lescale, while always having been a godsend for him, an attentive mentor, and in some respects a substitute father, was not a man who was always sensitive to the needs of his fellow human beings, and in this case, particularly women.

Once he had her trunk brought to the carriage, he helped Miss Lescale ascend. She wore no gloves, but he could feel she had a substantially firm grip for a lady. That was good. He suspected keenly that she would need fortitude to embrace this particular life adjustment. As he settled in next to her in the front seat and took up the reins, she spoke hesitantly. "Do you want your coat back now?"

"No, keep it until we get to the house. I don't want you to take a chill."

✣

They did not speak to each other a great deal. And it was most likely her fault, but she was quite exhausted, simply drained from the voyage and the preceding events.

"My dear, please do stay in touch and know you will always have a home here at Belle Coeur." Her aunt's eyes had been brimming with tears at her departure, but Emmeline gave no credit to that. Her experience of Aunt Adeleine was that she could summon such emotion at will, which could quickly dissipate just as easily.

As she and James Fallon slowly traveled through the streets of this strange new city, her eyes scarcely took in the sights around her. She was so weighed down with processing the turmoil of her inner recollections.

"You are so quiet, Miss Lescale. Are you well?"

"I am tired, Mr. Fallon. It has been a trying day."

There was a pause and then, "I completely understand, but if you feel it may be more than that, I might be able to help. I am a physician."

She glanced with surprise at the man seated next to her, his profile forward, intent on guiding the chestnut-colored horse pulling their gig. "I see," she replied softly. "So, it is Dr. Fallon."

A slight smile flickered across his lips, and she looked away. She certainly didn't want to be caught staring. "Yes, and if you desire, I can tend to you, Miss Lescale." Now this comment made her feel rather strange. The words were innocuous, even attentive, but there seemed an odd sort of imbalance somewhere, as though there were some hidden, buried intent that surely would not be apparent to any rational mind. Then again, she was so terribly exhausted and no doubt making inferences where there were none to be made.

"Do you know Nathaniel Lescale well, Dr. Fallon?" she asked with purpose.

"Yes, I would say so," he answered.

"May I ask you something?" It was impulsive, and she was unsure if she should broach anything with this virtual stranger.

"Of course."

"Why, why do you think after so many years of indifference, in fact virtual neglect, clearly for so many years forgetting my very existence, does this man now feel such a profound need for my presence?"

He was silent, and then she heard him sigh a bit in response to the rough tumble of words she'd expelled. Oddly, she could almost feel an unease pass through his frame, which was easy to do as he was seated so near her that their clothing was touching. "I see you are bitter," he murmured.

"Being bitter would imply some investment of emotion. Nathaniel Lescale is a stranger to me, Dr. Fallon. All I can invest toward him is a judgment of his actions. I have been cast out from an existence that I was familiar with and thrust into one that I am convinced will be quite unnatural for me." She took in a sharp breath. Of course, she'd lied, and it would not be hard to see the level of vitriol that seemed to be uncontrollably pouring out of her. Usually, she possessed more self-control, but perhaps the fatigue and the ugly, swift turn of events had proved too much for even her usual evenly measured nature.

But somewhat gallantly, she supposed, he showed no reflection of her sharpness in his answer. "Perhaps you should not prejudge things so harshly, Miss Lescale. I have always found it is better to allow life to unfold without forcing it to conform to expectations. Besides, surely you could have stayed with your aunt if that is what you truly wished."

"No, no, that is just the point, I couldn't. Something happened, some unknown pressure was applied, and then everything changed. My aunt and her son-in-law, Mr. Dufour, encouraged me to leave at the end. It became more than clear that I could no longer consider Belle Coeur my home." She'd answered emphatically, strenuously dismissing the vision of her aunt's teary face in her mind. After all, what Adeleine Le Maire said and what she meant had always been very distinctly separate.

"I see," he responded rather measuredly, "and you are unhappy about it."

She could feel the icy fire rising in her face. How she wished that she were as detached as she claimed to be. But acknowledged or not, there was a fury inside her trying to claw its way out. "I don't understand why that would be surprising. I don't enjoy being moved around and used like a pawn in someone else's chess game," she nearly snapped out. The doctor beside her smiled at the comment, which only served to further incense her. "I am so grateful, Dr. Fallon, that you find my present predicament amusing."

And then, quickly, he responded, "Please forgive me, Miss Lescale if I gave that impression. I was just enjoying your mental acuity. I rather appreciate the way your mind works. And in answer to your questions, I cannot claim to be privy to all of Dr. Lescale's private matters, nor would I wish to suggest that I am in any way supportive of his actions. It is my understanding that he felt convinced leaving you in the care of your relatives was in your best interest when you were young, and now, as circumstances are shifting, he feels it is in your best interest that you are here now."

She turned away, determined to hide her emotion. "As I expressed before, Dr. Fallon, a pawn in someone else's chess game."

"Well, it is my sincere hope that your opinion shifts over time."

"Can it really be of any consequence to you, Dr. Fallon?"

And curiously, there was no hesitation in his response. "Yes, actually, Miss Lescale, in many ways, it truly is."

Chapter 4

Nathaniel

Her eyes were wide open in the semidarkness of the room as she stared somewhat blindly at the low arching ceiling over her bed. The room itself was pleasant enough, not nearly as large as the one she had occupied at Belle Coeur, but then again, that had been an attic room, somewhat removed from the heart of the house. But here she was only several doors away from Nathaniel Lescale's master suite.

The bed she lay in had a headboard and footboard that were of an ironwork construction but delicate, capped with pale ivory ceramic ornamentation.

And the colors around her were light, ecru, feminine laces incorporated into the bedspread, as were the flowery ceramic bowls and vases placed strategically on the heavy, dark dresser and armoire.

Clearly, this room had been furnished with a female in mind. She shifted restlessly. Her trunk lay open at the foot of the bed. The maid — what was her name again — Mattie? That was it. Mattie Hart, a young red-haired girl of Irish descent, had promised to help her unpack in the morning. Mattie was married to the manservant, who seemed at first glance to be perhaps a decade or more her senior. Benjamin, that was it, Benjamin and Mattie Hart.

She had gleaned from them that there was no actual housekeeper. Her heart felt heavy. Perhaps that was the role her dear father had in mind for her. Nothing, none of it was clear. She and Dr. Fallon had arrived at the Esplanade Street house earlier in the evening. Dr. Fallon's gig was tended to by Benjamin as they walked onto a long wooden porch and then into the front entranceway.

It was all so foreign to her. Here, in the city, the houses were constructed so close together, not all the spacious land that surrounded Belle Coeur. "Is this where he lives?" she'd murmured to Dr. Fallon.

"Yes," he responded lightly as they were being greeted warmly by Mattie, who led them buoyantly into a small foyer.

As she followed Mattie Hart with Dr. Fallon closely behind into some sort of spacious parlor, Emmeline scarcely had a moment to absorb her surroundings when a tall, dark-haired man, though hair streaked generously with gray, entered from another doorway. He was smaller than Dr. Fallon, thinner, yet bearded as well.

He also wore a dark suit but with his tie undone and the suit itself, she noted, a bit wrinkled. But then, in her former circumstances, Emmeline had been taught to have an eye for such domestic details. He moved quickly and was standing in front of them before she even had a moment to draw breath.

"You are so fair, my dear, fragile like your mother," he said with a familiarity that prickled her immensely.

"Sir, surely you know nothing about me," she answered a bit too sternly, perhaps. "Fragility is the furthest thing from my nature."

However, it was immediately apparent that her cold pronouncement did not achieve the desired effect. The man, whom she had assumed was her neglectful father, smiled as though quite pleased. "Very good. That spirit will serve you well, Emma."

She frowned at the strange aberration of her name that he'd used.

Abruptly, he jovially slapped her traveling companion on the shoulder. "Thank you, Jack, for seeing her safely home."

And then she bristled further at the word home, but again she was undeniably determined to be displeased. Because, as it was in her estimation, she'd been virtually kidnapped, ripped from her former life, and forced to come here.

"Of course, Nathaniel, but I believe Miss Lescale might be in need of some food and rest. It's been a trying day for her."

Her father's dark brown eyes darted back to her as though suddenly alerted to the realization that this reunion might just be less than amiable for her. "Oh, well, of course. Are you all right, my dear?"

"I'm quite tired," she said curtly. "Perhaps I could be shown to my room."

And rather quickly, Mattie had taken her upstairs and brought her a bowl of soup before bed. Overwhelming did seem such an inadequate description for all of this. She wondered despondently what tomorrow would bring.

Perhaps it was possible that she could still get her father's or even Dr. Fallon's help in securing a position as a governess somewhere, anywhere else. She would certainly not stay here and be forced to take up some menial position of servitude at this man's house. It was different with her aunt. She had not been a servant but instead more of a personal companion. There were household matters she attended to that Aunt Adeleine preferred not to be bothered with. But Emmeline did them out of gratitude. She was grateful, she told herself, for a place to stay after being cast out by her own.

Here, in contrast, it was not the same at all. She owed nothing to her father, Nathaniel Lescale. He had abandoned her, without compunction she convinced herself, mentally dismissing all of his letters that had been kept from her. He'd left her when —

Then she stopped. She was so irate, in truth so hurt. How strange that she'd convinced herself she was devoid of these emotions. It seemed now that they had always been there, just put away, far away where they could not cause concern or more likely upset.

✢

"She's angry."

"Did you really expect that she wouldn't be?"

"Lissette was not like that. She was delicate, supportive."

"Emma is not her mother. She is a unique individual." Jack stood by the fireplace in Nathaniel's study, taking a sip of brandy from the glass he'd poured for himself moments before, then placing it on the dark walnut mantel of the fireplace.

"What impression do you get of her, Jack?"

He stared across Nathaniel's study at the older man, recognizing that his friend craved reassurance. Nathaniel Lescale was a brilliant chemist and respected doctor, with gifts and contributions in the field of scientific exploration that he would never be properly recognized for in his lifetime. But here, here in the sphere of familial relations, he was profoundly untried, and more than that, the truth was that Jack knew he didn't want to be bothered by it. Jack could be kind and lie to him, but their relationship had never been based on deception.

"My impression is that she's intelligent and very complicated. Don't expect to have an easy time here."

Nathaniel grumbled a bit, sinking down onto the couch. "Too much to hope for an old man to have a little peace."

"You aren't that old, my friend. And if you wanted peace, I suppose, you should have left things well enough alone."

Nathaniel frowned, sipping his brandy. Jack could tell that his friend seemed confused about the matter of his daughter. And whether Nathaniel would acknowledge it or not, Jack had exerted some of his influence to have Emma brought here. Nathaniel was unquestionably in a sort of decline, and he felt her

24

presence would be a help now. "Do you like her, Jack?" a question that seemed to come somewhat out of nowhere.

Jack Fallon considered for a moment. His thought process was analytical, as he'd been rigorously trained to be within his profession. But beyond that, there was another side to him, a wild, impetuous side of his nature that he'd worked hard to rein in at times.

"Honestly, I can't say yet. I don't know her well enough."

"Do you find her beautiful?" Now, this was different, an unexpected question, but then Nathaniel was taken to directness.

But how exactly to answer? Jack was undeniably drawn to beauty, but not what one would call obvious beauty. He could find beauty in aberration, in unexpected combinations, in short, not in the harmonious but in the inharmonious.

The image of Emmeline Lescale rose in his mind. Petite, though tall, well-formed, feminine figure, although on the thin side. Delicate bone structure, thick blonde hair, and the eyes — wide, almond-shaped but full of sparks — sparks of simmering, well-repressed emotion. How tantalizing a thought to ignite those well-controlled sparks and see how they'd burn.

"Yes," he said abruptly. He'd decided in an instant that he indeed found her beautiful.

"You should marry her, Jack. You need a wife."

He laughed shortly because that was all he could do at the moment. So instead, he answered off-handedly, "Nathaniel, I think perhaps it might be cruel to inflict any woman with a husband such as I would be."

⚜

It was difficult to sleep that night, and as it was, she was not at all sure if she did. The surroundings were so different, so different from her large attic bedroom at her aunt's house at Belle Coeur, though if she were honest, that place had its own formidable shadows. But her room had been different, different from the rest of that great manor. Although isolated in many respects, it had become a private refuge of sorts. There she would escape her somewhat regimented life into her domain, a place of books, painting, writing, and dreaming, dreaming of another, a kinder sort of existence. It was fancifulness indeed and perhaps the only place she allowed herself to indulge in such whimsy.

But here, here was a dramatically divergent sort of place, and in most respects, if she were to be truthful with herself, which she did endeavor to do, she was afraid. At the very least, the unhappiness and dissatisfaction she knew in her life at Belle Coeur were familiar, a known torment.

Here was nothing substantial that she could touch, lay her hands upon. It was an unnatural landscape. She squeezed her eyes shut, trying to calm herself. Where was the little girl who yearned for adventure or the young woman who ached for something of her own?

"Emma."

A whisper in the air was so light it must have come from somewhere else, perhaps a dream. *"My dearest one,"* the velvety voice again.

Slowly, her eyes opened in the semidarkness. And through the shadows, she could see a figure just standing at the foot of her bed. She should be frightened at the intrusion, but the feeling, just seeing her emanated a soothing calm. She was a lovely, slight, blonde woman in a long, light blue dress, smiling at her as though they were well acquainted. *"Don't be afraid, Emma,"* she whispered soothingly. *"I'm always with you, my darling."*

And then her eyes flickered closed, just for an instant, and when they reopened, the lady was gone. It wasn't until the morning that she remembered the nocturnal visit, and she fully acknowledged the truth. She recalled the resemblance the mysterious figure from her dream had to the portrait from Belle Coeur. Undeniably, the lady in the blue dress had been her long lost mother, Lizette.

Chapter 5

Bienville Street

It was approaching ten in the evening when Jack left Nathaniel Lescale's residence on Esplanade Avenue. He'd delayed his departure for a while, wanting to ensure that Emma was properly settled in for the night. He was concerned about her. She seemed too upset. Of course, this was to be expected, given the circumstances. But it bothered him, nonetheless.

The streets seemed largely silent as he drove his carriage to Bienville Street, where he resided. His home was a three-story porte-cochere townhouse. The structure itself was a bit deceptive at first viewing — a brick building with its gabled roof connected to other buildings at the side, forming a continuous facade along the street level. But within, the townhouse was much larger and more complicated than one might suppose. Directing his horses into the long, semi-circular, arched carriageway at the side entrance, they headed toward the back. Here, there was an extensive rear courtyard flanked by stables, a kitchen, a wash building, and a two-story garçonnière or young men's house, as it was called in the old Creole days.

Here, Jack kept two servants on intermittently to help him keep up with household maintenance, but only part of the time.

Most often, it was only him rambling through the great place, which at the moment suited him because he did value his privacy. And, of course, in addition, the great brick wall flanking the courtyard helped in that regard, keeping this patio secluded and protected from the view of curious neighbors.

Once the horse was situated in the stable, he traveled the outer staircase to the second floor. The rooms spanned the entire width of the building. Full-length galleries along the courtyard provided access to both the first and second stories. Within the house upstairs, there were bedrooms and a study that doubled as a parlor when he did entertain, seldom as that had proved to be. He left his jacket on a chair near the entrance and made his way down the hallway.

He really needed sleep. In the morning were rounds at the city hospitals, the Hotel Dieu and Charity. But he knew himself well enough to know that sleep would elude him for some time yet.

"You should marry her, Jack. You need a wife."

Nathaniel's words resounded in his mind. So odd for this to come up so quickly. After all, Emma Lescale had just arrived in New Orleans. But the old man was deeply perceptive without realizing it at all and connected, so connected to the heart of things. He poured himself a second brandy. The first, he hadn't finished at Nathaniel's house. He had a headache now, and he was more than sure this wouldn't be helpful, but tonight unquestionably was a unique evening. Because finally, after all this time, he had officially met Emma, well, Emma of the present anyway.

As he settled into a chair near the sofa, he noted that the house creaked around him with subtle and unidentifiable noises. It was an old place built close to a century before, although extensively remodeled after the city fire in 1794, but this was to be expected. There was history here, history that permeated the very walls of this place, and of course, that had been one aspect that undeniably had drawn him initially. He had been living here just three years now, and the house was much too large for a bachelor like himself. But when he bought it, he had his eye on the future. After all, life could change quickly and unexpectedly. This was a lesson he'd learned painfully in his youth. There was no question, however, that his Bienville Street address was important, essential in fact. He had recognized how crucial it would be to him long before he'd acquired it. He'd always known acutely that this was no ordinary structure.

"This city is very unique. People haven't just been drawn here for its congenial environment. There's a power here, power that can be tapped into."

Nathaniel had stressed this fact to him many years before he had even found the house on Bienville. In fact, it was also some time before he had become privy to many of Nathaniel's extracurricular interests beyond his expertise in physiological research.

He leaned his head backward on the chair because he was exceptionally weary. He'd expended much energy tonight. She was distraught, traumatized in some regards, he might even say. And he had sought to soften this harsh descent into a new life for her, tried, although how successfully, if at all, he couldn't truly say. He placed the brandy on an end table and closed his eyes, trying to summon the will to retire for the evening.

But then he heard them — footsteps, light footsteps just behind him. Distantly, he acknowledged that there was no one in the house except himself. But that caused him no alarm. After all, he was alone only at present.

Her voice was soft, nearly a whisper. "Difficult evening, Jack?"

He swallowed, breathing in deeply then answering smoothly without hesitation, "In some ways."

She glided nearly soundlessly across the wooden floor and sat quietly in the burgundy Bergere chair next to him.

He opened his eyes. It stunned him. Rather, she never failed to stun him. He smiled at her warmly but did not take her hand. Why? He wasn't sure. He didn't sense any danger except that he always attempted to keep a bit of distance during these occurrences, a bit of a separation between his life and this. He had to admit that she seemed even more beautiful to him now than she had earlier in the evening — calmer, more peaceful. Her blonde hair was long, undressed, and she wore a simple cotton nightgown covered by an intricate paisley shawl that covered her shoulders. Just into her thirties, he would estimate.

She smiled, looking a bit concerned. "Can I help you with anything?"

He laughed softly, not genuinely willing to absorb the irony of the situation. Could she help him with, well, navigating herself? "Explain to me how your mind worked long ago when you first came to this city."

She looked at him oddly with amusement, perhaps. Did he amuse her? Would he? "Much as it does now, only I was more ready to battle then, frightened, defensive. I found it difficult to trust, you see."

He tried to absorb what she was saying, but the truth was that he was so exhausted that not very much was being absorbed. "And how was I?"

Again, she smiled a bit, though elusively, as though she were keeping a secret from him. Then she glanced back to the doorway. "I have to go now, Jack. I hear someone calling."

"You didn't answer me," he said a bit groggily because now he knew he would sleep tonight after all.

"No, I didn't," she said before she left.

⚜

Emma Fallon silently walked through the house she'd lived in for the last seven years. As she wandered barefoot on plush throw rugs covering the wooden floor of the hallway, she felt a familiar rush of dizziness pass through her. She steadied herself with a hand bracing against the wall, knowing fully from experience that the moment would pass.

She breathed in deeply, schooling herself to allow stillness within from her innermost thoughts to her outermost skin. It was like a storm roaring in her ears, a sound so encompassing that it would be quite easy to be overtaken by it.

Holding onto the calmness within, she remembered one of the early times when the phenomenon had first occurred. Back then, she'd had no idea what was happening, and Jack, her husband now, had not yet been forthcoming about his life, and particularly this home. Then it had been quite terrifying, but now, well, now it was just a part of their everyday existence.

Stealthily, she opened the doorway to their bedroom, hoping fervently that her nocturnal journey hadn't disturbed her husband, as it, at present, was a point of contention between them. That particular hope was quickly extinguished as he was sitting up waiting for her in the great cherry wood four-poster bed, the room illuminated by an oil lamp that he'd lit on a nearby night table. It was not hard for her to tell immediately that he was a bit irritated but so had been the nature of their relationship. He would try to set parameters — to, in his own words, *"keep her safe and protected,"* — and she would listen, then follow her mind.

Throughout their eventful six-year marriage, she'd felt that they had made progress on that front. But then the baby changed everything. It had brought out his former fiercely protective nature.

"Did you hear me call you, Emma?" He asked with little emotion, with little emotion but with plenty of it churning up beneath the surface.

She smiled at him, pulling her paisley shawl more tightly around her. "I did, though distantly, Jack. And I came as soon as I heard you." She would soothe him. She was willing to do that, but only to a degree.

"But it still took you some time to return. Where were you?"

"In the parlor," she said calmly. After all, it was the truth.

"And who was with you?" he asked slowly with deliberation in his voice.

Her eyes widened, but she shouldn't be surprised. He knew. Of course, he did. Moving between always left its residue, and he was so damned perceptive. "Who?" she repeated his inquiry, still standing quietly at the foot of the four-poster bed.

"Yes, who?"

She smiled a bit endearingly and said sweetly with a tinge of flirtatiousness. "Why, Jack, are you jealous?"

His blue-gray eyes hardened a notch. Evidently, this wasn't the tack to take. "Emma," he said in a low but somewhat steely voice. "I would appreciate an answer."

"You would appreciate one, or are you insisting on one? You know when you married me that the restrictions of this institution would not bind me."

"And have you been?" he answered softly.

"No, but—" and her protestations felt weak in this particularly stringent moment they seemed stuck in. "Of course, I was with you."

He nodded, saying nothing for a moment. Naturally, he'd known that from the beginning. "You are taking risks, especially with —"

"Yes, yes, I know, the baby. After two miscarriages, there is slim chance that I can produce a healthy child."

He sighed, not really audibly, but she could hear it somewhere around her heart. "I didn't marry you so that you could produce children, Emma. You seemed as though this is what you wanted."

Her breath hitched a bit as the truth of his words caught up with her. Now there were tears in her throat, filling her eyes, threatening to engulf this whole mess. At times, it felt intolerable to go through all that again, the anticipation and then the abysmal disappointment and loss that felt like it just might drain all the life out of the world. And here she was, pregnant for the third time — only knowing that she couldn't function wrapped up in so much fear that she might take a false step and somehow inadvertently bring on calamity.

She shook her head. "I honestly don't know what I want anymore."

He swung his legs over the side of the bed. He wore a long nightshirt and a plush dark blue Indian robe. "Why did you feel it was important to travel now, Emma?"

She shrugged, still struggling to beat down the fierce and warring emotions that were bubbling up. "You know it's not always so controllable, Jack. But I felt something so strong — a need." She moved closer to him. "Can you remember me? Like I was when we first met?"

His eyes took on a different quality, the same look as when he'd finally put the pieces of something together. "Yes, of course, I do."

She murmured, "You seemed a bit lost."

He held out his hand to her, which she took readily. "You have always anchored me, Emma."

She moved into his warm embrace that comforted and gave her strength.

"But what might have happened if we hadn't come together, Jack?"

"Come to bed," he said with gravity. It was clear that he wouldn't be discussing this possibility anymore tonight.

Chapter Six

Her Father's House

There was plenty for her to do in the house on Esplanade Avenue, a reality Emmeline gleaned the first week she was there. The main house was quite different from her aunt's at Belle Coeur, besides lacking in acreage. Though, as of late, much of Aunt Adelaine's grounds had been taken up in crop planting or sold off to cover increasing debts. Her father's, or rather Nathaniel's, home on Esplanade Avenue was much smaller, less airy, and not nearly as private as the sprawling Belle Coeur. And in total, her father employed only the two servants, Mattie and Benjamin Hart, who lived downstairs in the back of the residence.

Emmeline's bedroom was upstairs, just beyond her father's room, and on the other side of the central stairwell was a dining room that seemed rarely used as she and her father took their meals separately. She had noted rather quickly that Nathaniel spent much of his time in his study, even on occasion sleeping there on the chaise lounge positioned against the wall. Upstairs, across the hallway from her room, there was a second, smaller parlor her father indicated she could use as a private sitting area if she wished. This was a deference she wasn't expecting. There had been only one sort of attic-level room for her at Belle Coeur.

Although it was spacious, it was somewhat sparse in furnishings compared to the accommodations afforded the La Maire girls. Here, oddly, she was now the mistress of the house, an uncomfortable designation for her, to say the least.

In addition, there was a one-story outbuilding on the side of a rather unkept garden, partially brick-laid, partially earth. This, however, did bother her. The grounds at Belle Coeur were so beautifully well-tended. Emmeline herself had spent much time in them, pruning rose bushes and helping to tend a garden whose vegetables and herbs were often used in the kitchen. Outside of the library, it had always been her favorite place to be. But here, what should be a garden was neglected. If she were to stay, a possibility she found doubtful, she would have to change this and make it her own. The outbuilding in the back, curiously though, seemed to serve many purposes. In addition to being a kitchen, it was also some manner of laboratory for what Mattie termed Mr. Nathaniel's experiments, as he'd stopped practicing as a physician some years back.

From what Emmeline gathered, her father now spent his time publishing in medical journals and consulting. However, in inquiring in what capacity exactly, Emmeline found that she was met with vagueness.

"So, what exactly is your income?" Emmeline had asked him one day in a decidedly not very delicate manner.

Nathaniel Lescale was in his study, rifling through a volume of what she could only identify as a very large, dusty, leather-bound book. He looked up a little befuddled as though her very presence was, at best, a distraction and, at worst, a nuisance. "It fluctuates, investments, my dear. Why do you ask?" he said, wrinkling his brow.

"It occurs to me that you could use a housekeeper or perhaps a cook."

He frowned as though some pesky insects were buzzing around his face. "Why? That would be a waste. Mattie and Benjamin do fine in that regard."

"I don't agree —" she had nearly addressed him as father, but at the moment, she'd begrudgingly decided that he did not deserve the title. "Things could be done much more efficiently."

Another distracted frown, she glanced back down at the book that he continued to focus on with frustration. She suspected it was handwritten, in a foreign language, French perhaps, but she wasn't quite sure. Adeleine La Maire had thought that her daughters should learn French, as her family was of a Creole tradition. But she hadn't insisted, and their father Henry spoke it only to select old acquaintances in Vacherie. And regrettably, Emmeline hadn't taken the time to learn, although now she wondered if she should have.

Her attention returned to Nathaniel. His glasses, she could see, were smudgy, and his desk, in general, was cluttered with papers, books, and other extraneous items with dust, far too much dust. No wonder he struggled with concentration. She dismissed the thought outright that, in this particular instance, she might be the problem.

"My dear Emma," he said in a slightly grumbling voice. "We must live within our means. But I give you leave to manage things. Bring on no new servants but take Mattie and Benjamin in hand as you like."

She frowned for a number of reasons. One was his continued use of the name Emma. She had corrected him on that once, no, maybe twice. He'd replied with obstinacy that her mother, Lizette, had always referred to her as Emma, although admittedly, she'd spent an inordinately brief amount of time with her. And secondly, the idea of taking over the management of this house with no additional help — what a lot of work that would be. Perhaps, she thought dimly, she should revisit the possibility of hiring herself out as a governess. "Very well," she murmured because she could not think of what else to say. And with very little encouragement, Nathaniel returned his full attention to his old dusty book. She wondered dismally, and not for the first time, why he'd insisted she come here. Clearly, he seemed to have such little interest in her presence.

Of course, in all of the house, the little garden area or courtyard, as Mattie termed it, was her favorite place. With Mattie and Benjamin's help, she did clear it of debris, damaged tools, parts of an old carriage, broken pieces of furniture, and had placed out a lovely set of wrought black iron furniture that she had found in one of the old storage rooms off the kitchen.

And as she could, she made plans to landscape it, fill it with flowers, roses particularly, maybe a trellis or gazebo of some sort. She had great intentions for the space. That was again, if indeed she decided to stay.

For Emmeline, the idea of making it her own intrigued her. She seemed to be the only one who frequented the secluded area. And it was on one such occasion in her first month of residence in her father's home that Dr. Fallon found her there.

"Miss Lescale, what a pleasure."

She had noticed that Dr. Fallon had entered the courtyard from a side entrance of the house. He was dressed in his usual wardrobe, dark gray suit, and hat, while she wore a simple morning outfit — a long gray skirt with a fitted ivory blouse. Her hair was pulled up in her usual no-nonsense style, a thick chignon bun at the base of her neck.

In her days at Belle Coeur, Pauline had often coaxed her to experiment with more intricate hairstyles, but her response had always been — "I never plan to marry little one, so why bother?"

In her weeks here on Esplanade Avenue, she had noted that Jack Fallon was a frequent visitor. There had always been cordial greetings between them, but mostly, his attention would be taken up by Nathaniel. Often, the two would vanish into the study and sometimes even have Mattie serve them dinner there. It was clear that there was some strong bond between the men, one that she clearly fell into the periphery of. That was until perhaps this moment.

She smiled as he approached, quickly closing the book in which she'd been writing. This was her journal, her most per-sonal thoughts, which she never intended to expose to anyone ever. One day, when she was very old, she thought she might burn it to ensure it never fell into undeserving hands. But that was too far into the future to consider in any definitive way.

She rose as he neared the table and took his hand that, as it was, had no glove today.

"Good to see you, Dr. Fallon," she said politely, then reseated herself. With no encouragement, he took the chair across from her. She was a bit surprised by this as, up until now, he'd never really sought out her company. Placing his bowler on the table, he smiled broadly at her. "I'm sure Nathaniel is in his study if you were looking for him."

"I wanted to stop by to see how you are settling in, and Mattie told me that you were outside enjoying the morning sun in the courtyard. I was pleased to hear it. I've always told Nathaniel that he keeps it woefully neglected."

She glanced around, feeling a bit puzzled by his shift of attention toward her. "Well, yes, it is a lovely space, or rather I think it could be under the proper care," she said haltingly.

Another engaging smile. "And you have plans for it?"

She glanced back toward the house a bit nervously. How direct his gaze was, so very different from the gentlemen in the circle of her aunt's acquaintance who never seemed willing to engage with her for any extended period. But then again, she had always suspected they did not consider her quite at their level, as she was unceremoniously viewed as simply her Aunt Adeleine's companion.

"Well, I don't know. Though I do think it could be made very nice."

"Then you should make it so, Emma. This place certainly needs someone to take charge."

And then she returned his gaze directly. "Is that why I was brought here, Dr. Fallon, to take charge?"

He smiled again, seeming in an odd mix of appreciation and being slightly uncomfortable at the inquiry. But he seemed to step out of that quagmire by smoothly deflecting, "How are you getting on with your father, Emma?"

"Nathaniel? I rarely see him. He spends his time in his study or in that other room in the back."

"I see," he said a bit pensively. "Nathaniel has become more reclusive as of late."

"Well, quite honestly, I really don't know why he wanted me here at all. It seems quite the mystery."

Then unexpectedly, he reached out and placed his hand over hers, which was resting on the wrought iron table. "You must believe me, Emma. He needs you here."

She pulled her hand away abruptly. Perhaps it was rude, but the contact and familiarity made her feel strange, unsettled, to say the least. Her skin still tingled from where he had touched her. "You know Dr. Fallon, my Christian name is Emmeline, and I don't understand why everyone here seems determined that I adopt the variation of Emma."

He frowned a bit at this. "I'm sorry. It's how I've always heard your father refer to you. Would you prefer Emmeline?"

Now, this did unsettle her. It was a question that she had not considered. Did she? The truth was that she'd never been overly fond of her name, and here was a peculiar opportunity to shed it altogether for something untried — her choice of how she was called, what a concept. "Actually, Dr. Fallon, I don't know. I have not considered it. When I was with my aunt at Belle Coeur, I seemed to be completely different, but now I'm not sure who I am to be. And as for Nathaniel, it is very difficult for me to see how he could truly want me here. Most of the time, my presence feels as though it is a nuisance to him."

"Well, perhaps a little patience and a little time, and as for your name, I will continue to call you Emma until you tell me not to. Because in a purely selfish way, I am fond of it."

She shifted a bit in the hard wrought iron chair, feeling oddly dissatisfied on the whole. It was clear to her that Dr. Fallon's allegiance was purely with her father.

"So, are you writing letters to your friends?" He indicated the leather-bound book she had closed upon his arrival.

The ink jar and pen sat plainly in sight on the table. "No, it's just a journal. I'm a chronicler of sorts. I've left no friends that I intend to correspond with."

"Really, none, Emma?" And there it was again. He was as good as his word, seeming quite comfortable using that name. In a way, it felt like a liberty of some sort. But again, he seemed so affable when he did it that she found it challenging to take serious offense. "That sounds lonely."

She looked at him pointedly. Why was he interested? Was this a physician giving some attention to a potential patient? No one usually took so much time in inquiring after her interests, her plans, thoughts, not ever. She answered concisely. "It is the way it is. My nature is solitary, I suppose."

There was something there in his eyes as though he was intently absorbing what she said. "Yes, I can understand that, but at some point, connections can be considered worthwhile, perhaps desirable."

She straightened up a bit. "I have no experience with what you are speaking of, Dr. Fallon."

He nodded as though brushing away the intensity of the moment. "I have brought my carriage. I thought perhaps we could ride about the city a bit and then have lunch."

She felt a bit startled and taken aback at his pronouncement. "Really, today?"

"Yes, I'll wait while you get ready. Sorry, I gave you no notice, but some time opened up unexpectedly for me this morning." And then he added smoothly, "And I would greatly enjoy your company."

Of course, she should refuse. Her aunt would have advised her to rebuff his offer soundly. It was clear in this invitation that Dr. Fallon was not observing any decorum. Then again, she was beginning to comprehend that this was a different world from the house at Vacherie, and she would have to learn its rules. After a hesitation, she answered, "Yes, Dr. Fallon, that would be very nice, thank you. I'll just get my things."

"And Emma," he stated abruptly, stopping her mid-stride as she was approaching the entrance into the house.

"Yes," she said, holding the journal she'd gathered up close to her chest.

"I would be delighted if you would call me Jack. Dr. Fallon feels terribly formal."

"Well, I will certainly try," she said quickly, feeling just a bit flushed and caught off guard by the request, before she headed inside.

Chapter 7

An Outing

Emmeline had refreshed her appearance just a bit, putting on a jacket bodice matching her long gray skirt and the bonnet that Aunt Adeleine had bought for her last Christmas. It occurred to her, staring at the reflection in the long rosewood cheval mirror, that her wardrobe was very sedate for someone her age. After all, she wasn't in mourning, but she had always gravitated to subdued shades. Of course, she had never been one to try to draw attention to herself, and life at Belle Coeur had made that somewhat of a necessity. So being adequately satisfied with her appearance, she headed downstairs to meet Dr. — no, correcting herself — Jack. After all, it wouldn't do to be rude to the first hand of friendship that had been offered in this new life.

✝

"You know, you might make more of an effort with her, Nathaniel."

His friend grumbled rather rudely in his direction. There was no doubt a change occurring within his mentor more quickly than Jack had anticipated.

"I don't know why you insisted she come here, Jack. She is making Benjamin and Mattie very nervous with all her demands." Nathaniel continued to rifle through the papers on his desk absently.

"Change isn't always a bad thing, old man. You've been pretty stagnant here. Perhaps Emma can breathe some fresh air into the place." He'd always used the term old man congenially with Nathaniel just to pull him out of his tendency to stuffiness. But Jack was worried about him and, more than anything, worried that he would be driving Emma away with the pitchfork of his brittleness before she even had a chance to acclimate.

"You know, Lizzie was never like this. She always knew when to leave well enough alone."

"Emma is not her mother. She is unique." He added on a bit more softly than he'd intended.

And with that, Nathaniel stopped for a moment with the papers. His dark eyes narrowed in on Jack in a manner he remembered from long ago. "Seems like you were the one who really wanted her here. I was willing to leave well enough alone."

Jack felt a coldness pass through him. He wasn't oblivious to the narcissistic tendencies his friend tended to display from time to time. "She is your daughter, Nathaniel. Don't you owe her some consideration?"

"Well, seems as though you believe I do."

⚜

"Don't you have work today?"

"No, no patients today. I made rounds at the Hotel Dieu this morning, but was going to spend the afternoon working on research at my home."

"But instead, you're helping me plant my garden."

They'd spent some time riding through the city and then lunching at a small cafe on the edge of the French Quarter. It had been a relaxing interlude of light conversation as Jack slowly watched Emma Lescale begin to relax into quite an entrancing young woman. She'd even genuinely smiled a few times, making him think of many things — one being that he'd like to see her in something other than gray.

Then, a curious moment presented itself as they were sitting on the patio of the Cafe Du Monde. An area of discussion came up rather quickly that Jack had not anticipated.

"I had a dream," Emma said somewhat out of the blue.

"Really? What was it about?"

She smiled briefly, nervously, never for too long. Guarded was a description that seemed inadequate to the barriers she appeared intent on encasing herself within. "You'll think I'm odd."

"Well, for my taste, I have to say that I find odd more than a bit compelling."

She sipped her coffee, seeming tentative to continue. "All right then, it was on that first night in Nathaniel's house."

Whenever she referred to the Esplanade home, he noticed that it was always *Nathaniel's house* — detaching herself somewhat and most definitely avoiding the word father.

"What happened?" he prodded, feeling intrinsically that this disclosure from her might somehow be significant.

"It was in the bedroom, where I sleep. But I was awake, or it felt like I was. Well, you see, a woman was standing in front of the doorway, and she was talking to me."

"What did she say?" he asked softly.

"That's what's odd or part of it. I can't remember. It seemed important, but I can't remember now. But she looked familiar, then later I understood." He waited, feeling it was best for her to unravel this in her own time. "I understood that she looked like me and, of course, a portrait that was at Belle Coeur. I believe it was my mother and that she was trying to tell me something important," she laughed shortly, almost as though embarrassed by what she'd said. "Do you think that's madness?"

No," he answered, "no Emma, I don't. I suppose you could say my beliefs, truths if you wish, are a bit less predictable than someone you would normally find in my profession."

"I'm not sure I understand what you mean," but she was eying him with curiosity.

"Beyond what could be considered empirical science is another realm of thought, vastly unexplored, at least not publicly so. Suffice to say that what you experienced, I am more than certain, was no dream. It was most definitely a contact."

"A contact?"

"Yes, your mother was clearly reaching out to you."

She glanced away as though she were made uncomfortable by his declaration. Quite certainly, he held many, many views that most would find unorthodox, to say the least. But then the conversation shifted to more earthly matters like his practice, his patients. He knew that he'd made her nervous, so he allowed her to awkwardly change the subject with no protestation on his part.

✢

Their outing had culminated in a stop at the French Market, a rather eclectic bazaar in the center of the city where they'd acquired the shrubbery for her intended transformation of Nathaniel's courtyard. "So, your father knew Nathaniel?"

"Yes, our mothers were acquainted. They were both French Creoles, you see, who came from the city here. In fact, my mother taught me French, which, it seems, is almost a necessity around here."

"My Aunt Adeleine spoke French. I always wanted to learn but never really took the time. But your father and Nathaniel—"

"Yes, well, my father was a surgeon during the war. He and Nathaniel began to correspond. Then, when my parents died, I began corresponding with him. I expressed an interest in studying medicine, and he offered to sponsor me if I moved down here."

"From where again?"

"Missouri, St. Louis, actually."

"Ah, a long way to come," she murmured. It was getting hot. They had acquired all manner of flowering plants in the French Market, and then, rather chivalrously, or so he intended, he had volunteered to help her plant them in the courtyard where the two of them had remained for some time. "What happened to your parents, Jack?"

"It was cholera. Spread as virulently as yellow fever did here. And you see, I was also afflicted, not expected to live."

She paused for a moment as though completely absorbing what he had said. "How terrible for you, so there really was nothing left for you there."

"No, your father became a lifeline for me. I moved here, my mother's former home, and studied at Tulane."

She smiled at him a little sadly, and he was shot deeply with the emotion of her suspected thoughts. He had received all the attention and devotion that her father had withheld from her. "Well, it is good that he could be there for you."

"You know winter is coming. You'll have to protect those plants, so they'll bloom in the spring."

"Yes, yes, you're right," she said with some preoccupation. It was clear that his revelations had dimmed her mood a bit. "Maybe Mattie can help me find something to make coverings with."

"Perhaps I can find something at my house."

She looked up with a little distraction. "Your house? Where is that?"

"Bienville Street," and then he added thoughtfully, "I'd like you to see it soon."

⚜

Jack Fallon had a curious way about him. He made her forget things, in particular that things were difficult for her and that she faced an uncertain future. He had a peculiar way of exuding a confidence in life that was contagious and insidious. And his belief in, now how did he put it, another realm of thought left her a bit unsettled and yet intrigued at the same time. In so many words, he'd implied that her mother's ghost was trying to speak to her. That didn't sit well with her pragmatic nature. But at times, she wondered if she was really that pragmatic or if it was just a ruse that she'd possibly played on herself. In any case, Jack Fallon was having a strange effect on her. She felt like a different Emmeline around him, perhaps this new persona, this Emma everyone seemed intent on making her into. Clearly, during the course of the afternoon, he was lulling her into a different mind-set. Distantly and less than comfortably, she wondered if this was what it felt like to be seduced.

The afternoon sun had warmed everything, including the brick-laid pavement of the patio, but she knew well by now that a chill would enshroud all her efforts in the evening.

"What sort of house is it?" she asked as she began to plant the first row of chrysanthemums along the garden bed.

"In size, a bit larger than your father's, I believe, although quite different in floor plan. It's a townhouse, three stories, nearly a hundred years old, I'd imagine, but with a carriageway along the side and stable beyond the courtyard." She had been on her knees bending over the new flowerbed, but now sat back on her legs, looking up at him intently.

"Such a substantial house for a single gentleman. Are you planning to have a large family one day, Dr. Fallon?" In the moment completely forgetting her promise to call him Jack.

He stood up from kneeling, dusting off his pants in the process. She glanced up at him. Perhaps it had been rude of her to ask such a personal question. But she didn't care. It was a sunny day, and she felt oddly hopeful that pleasantness was possible for her.

He pulled up one of the black wrought iron chairs closer to them and sat for a moment. "Yes, Miss Lescale, one day I would very much like a family."

She responded softly, "Yes, I imagine you would like that, given how you have lost your birth family."

"And what about you, Emma? Would you like a family of your own?"

His gaze was forthright in the inquiry, making her think perhaps this went beyond idle conversation. But that couldn't be true as they barely knew each other, so she looked away, firmly patting the warm earth around the freshly planted flowers. In general, however, it was an uncomfortable question because the idea of a family was comforting to her in some ways. Still, of course, other considerations came with it. "No, Dr. Fallon, I never intend to marry."

He stood and walked over to her, holding his hand out. She took it, allowing him to pull her easily to her feet. She noted the streaks of dirt all over her good skirt. No doubt she should have changed it before attempting this endeavor.

Looking up, she suddenly realized that he was still holding her hand. She peered into his gaze with question. "Why?"

"Why what?" she answered.

"Why do you never intend to marry?" She gently tugged at her hand, but he held it still somewhat firmly, making this a peculiarly intimate moment. His touch was warm and undeniably was sending sensations through her skin.

"Women lose all sense of freedom when they marry. I don't want to lose myself in someone else's life."

He smiled briefly. "That seems unlikely to me, Emma, particularly for you."

She pulled her hand back abruptly in a somewhat fierce tug. "I've been witness to it often enough."

He looked at her with some measure of contemplation, then said thoughtfully, "I wouldn't be so presumptuous as to try to talk you out of your beliefs, but I would very much like you to see my house. It is unique in some respects, and I certainly would like to know what you make of it."

She smiled, not really meaning to, but there was something about him, being around him, that put her into a different frame of mind. "I'd like that. So, will you help me plant the rest of these?" indicating the row of flowerpots he'd insisted on purchasing for her that still lay on the ground.

He nodded, "Absolutely, I do not like to leave a task unfinished, no matter how badly it damages my attire."

She laughed, for the moment allowing all other concerns to drift away.

Chapter 8

Voices

He was on her mind the rest of the day and the day after. She schooled herself soberly that he was just being kind to a daughter of an old friend. After all, Dr. Fallon, or Jack as he'd again reminded her to call him, was a considerate man, or so she believed.

Undeniably, their time together that day had brought a smile to her lips, a lift from somewhere inside her heart. She had made a friend, something that felt odd. She wasn't at all sure if she'd ever really had a friend before. Pauline, she supposed, but that was not an unguarded relationship. In whatever she said or whatever she did at Belle Coeur, Emmeline had to be conscious because she was playing a role. There was always a stress within her because of it. She consistently allowed her relatives to believe she was indeed who they wanted her to be.

But today, with Jack, it was different. She could not imagine that anything she expressed would cause him to reject her. Of course, she couldn't be sure if that was true, but without reservation, it certainly felt true. These were the thoughts floating unceremoniously around her mind this evening when she retired. And when she awoke, there was still darkness in the room, but she had heard a voice.

"Emma," muffled, and surely not in address to her but rather a word during a conversation.

She sat up, letting the covers fall down around her nightgown. She'd thought of the dream of her mother that she'd had when she first arrived. But this was not that soothing feeling at all. Glancing about, she felt an odd, inexplicable distortion of things, a strange sort of dizziness sweeping around her. She took a deep breath, trying to orient herself. Perhaps it was some slight illness that was making her feel unsteady. Swinging her feet over the side of the bed, again she felt shaky.

And outside the door, she heard it once more, unidentified people whispering loudly. *"No, Emma, surely not Emma."*

Then following, there were softer murmurs that were so low they seemed nearly inaudible to her.

A voice broke through that she recognized clearly to be Nathaniel's. "Lizette, where are you going? You must stay and help me with all of this." Without stopping to think, Emmeline sprang up, grabbed a shawl lying across the back of a nearby chair, and flung the door wide open. The narrow corridor was dimly lit by an oil lamp affixed to the wall, but it was empty, completely. Again, so very close, she heard a rush of heavy, loud whispers, but largely jumbled. It was undoubtedly Nathaniel's voice, but the other was soft, unidentifiable.

Quickly, she moved around the corner, barely seeing a glimpse of a figure disappearing down the staircase when her foot got jumbled up in the hem of her long cotton nightgown. A quick twist of pain made her lose her balance, stumble, and fall down the first few steps before the stairwell turned the corner. In dizziness, she slumped into a heap against the wall, feeling a sharp, jabbing pain around her knee.

Just lovely, she thought to herself with vexation as she weakly and painfully pulled herself to her feet. Out of nowhere, in only moments, Mattie, a bit disheveled, suddenly appeared from directly around the downstairs corner. Dressed in her nightgown and a wrap, her sky-blue eyes seemed enormous in the dim lighting. "Miss Emma, I heard a loud noise. Are you all right?"

"Yes, I stumbled, Mattie," she responded with frustration. "Did you see anyone else down there?"

"Down there?" she said with a bit of confusion. "Well, Benjamin got up and was looking around to see what happened, and as far as I know, Mr. Nathaniel is still asleep."

"Oh," she said, leaning against the wall, feeling a bit foolish, wondering for the first time if she'd been walking in her sleep or something of the like. "I thought I heard people outside my door."

"People, Miss?"

"Yes," she said slowly, realizing from Mattie's face that she sounded quite incoherent, but she was more than grateful for her help getting back to her room.

✣

It was early, in fact, too early, given the night's events, when Mattie knocked on the door stating that Dr. Fallon was waiting for her in the dining room. Dr. Fallon, at this hour? But then upon entering Mattie quickly informed her that she had sent a message to him early in the morning, asking him to check on Miss Emma before his rounds. At that, Mattie rapidly exited before Emmeline could work up the energy to chastise her. Well, that was all she needed after last night's debacle to feel foolish in front of Jack Fallon. She quickly finished getting dressed without Mattie's assistance before carefully navigating the stairs down to the first floor.

When she entered, Jack was waiting in the dining room, staring out the window onto the back patio. He was dressed in a dark suit, but she noted the black leather medical bag on the table. "Jack, I am surprised to see you here so early."

"Mattie sent me a note that you had a fall last night," he replied sternly. Or was that concern? Quite honestly, in her present state of mind, she found it challenging to sift through and determine.

"Oh yes," she felt a blush sweep her cheeks. Undeniably, she did feel off-balance. After going over the incident in her mind, she'd concluded that she'd been confused after a dream and had done a bit of overly dramatic sleepwalking. "It was just a bit of a stumble. It's nothing, really. I'm sorry that she dragged you here so early this morning."

He took her hand, gesturing for her to sit in a chair. "Well, indulge me. Since I'm here, do allow me to be of service. What exactly happened?"

"I, well, I woke up and thought I heard voices outside my room. But after thinking about it, I'm sure I must have been dreaming it all."

"What kind of voices?" he asked a bit gravely.

"At the time, it sounded like Nathaniel speaking to someone else, a woman, I thought. And then I believed I heard my name. So, I went into the hall and saw nothing, then went to the stairs and got a little tangled up and fell."

"Fell?"

"Yes, but nothing really serious, just that first flight, a few stairs — banged up my knee a bit."

He nodded pensively. "Is it still hurting?"

"My knee? Um, a bit, yes, just bruised, I'm sure."

"Well, since I'm here, let's see it."

Again, an unexpected blush swept over her as she reminded herself that Jack, indeed, was a medical physician. "Jack, I'm sure it's fine. I—"

"No reason to be shy, Emma. I am a doctor, right or left?"

"Right," she murmured uncomfortably. Without hesitation, he leaned over her chair and directly pushed her dark green skirt over her knee. Without even looking at her, he ran his hands up and down the front of her leg over her stockings, then peeled them down a bit to expose the kneecap and examine it thoroughly, as well as a bit up her thigh. The procedure felt so abrupt and unsettling as she repeatedly reminded herself that he was indeed a doctor and that the warmth and tingling spreading all over her leg from his touch was simply in her mind. It sprang from the imagination of a very inexperienced, sheltered young woman who had never been courted, kissed, or even considered by men in general. She firmly told herself that these sensations were simply fancifulness on her part, but it felt as though she was frozen in the moment as his strong hand continued relentlessly checking the bones of her leg.

"Doesn't seem to be any break," he murmured in a low voice. Then, putting one hand over the front of her leg and the other behind it, he applied a gentle pressure that only confused her further. His hands felt so strong and powerful, and she could genuinely feel a heat emanating from them. "I can wrap the knee if you feel you need something to support it."

She didn't answer, couldn't seem to at the moment. Then he looked up into her face from where he was kneeling. He had to see it. She knew he must. She was such a child reacting this way to simply having a doctor's hands on her. "No," she managed a little breathlessly. "It's all right."

And then there was that moment, an infinite stillness between them as his eyes continued to meet hers. She must have been wrong because otherwise, it felt as though it was an acknowledgment of the reaction his hands on her naked leg were eliciting in both of them.

There was that expression in his eyes that was hard to identify, perhaps curiosity, perhaps something else. But quite suddenly and deliberately, he removed his hands and pulled her skirt back into place. "The voices you heard, Emma, perhaps they were a dream."

She nodded quickly, trying to move past that odd and intractable moment. "Yes, yes, of course, that must have been." He stood then, holding his hand out for her as he brought her to her feet.

"You need to be careful, you know. You were lucky this wasn't serious."

"I will try Dr. — I mean, Jack. Perhaps, it's just all the change affecting me oddly."

Then she noticed he hadn't let go of her hand. "I have to go now. I have rounds at the hospital. But I'll check on you later. Try to rest a bit."

"Yes, I will," unsettling indeed. She smiled back at him because she couldn't help herself. It was almost as if he had willed it from her.

Chapter 9

West End

For almost an entire week after Emmeline's somewhat humiliating fall, Jack Fallon was nearly a constant visitor at the house on Esplanade Avenue. Some days, he arrived early in the morning, having breakfast before his hospital rounds, and at other times in the evening, visiting Nathaniel but also without fail her as well. He attentively inquired after her injury, which, as the days went by, didn't seem to be much of an injury at all. But she would smile and divert his attention from it. She didn't want a repeat of his rather exhaustive examination of her leg. The truth was she didn't want him touching her that way, physician or not. It had confused her, unsettled her, and made her think that there was something between them, something growing — something out of her control that she did not want to happen. So, she was friendly, cordial, and perhaps a bit distant, excusing herself at times. But he did make it difficult. Jack Fallon, she found, could be somewhat tenacious and possibly deter-mined beneath his affable exterior.

"How are you feeling, Emma?"

"Fine," she'd answered.

"No repercussions with the leg?"

"No, it seems to have healed quite nicely."

She returned her attention to the book she was reading. It was a collection of poetry from Pauline that she'd sent by parcel post. It had been one of Emma's favorite books that she had read many times. Pauline had pulled it from the library shelves at Belle Coeur, citing the fact that her mother rarely ever went into that room. In the same correspondence, Pauline also promised that she and Charles would come to see her at the beginning of December before Christmas.

She glanced up, surprised to find that Jack Fallon was still watching her intently on the other side of the black wrought iron table. She closed the book slowly, wondering why he hadn't left. "Was there something else, Dr. Fallon?"

He was studying her and possibly frowning, she thought, though she really couldn't be sure. "Yes, I think there is."

She waited, looking at him a bit quizzically, but he hadn't elaborated. "Not concerning my knee, surely?"

"Not directly," he said.

"Oh," she managed, lightly tapping the hard cover of the black volume that she was more than anxious to resume reading. The truth was that Pauline's gesture deeply touched her, and she dearly wanted to return to the book. It elicited comforting memories of roaming through the great collection of books at Belle Coeur. It was one of the rooms there that truly felt, and she hesitated in her description, "safe" to her there. She would slip silently into the comforting space with its dark furniture, walls layered with bookshelves, and a fireplace that was often lit in the winter. And there she would lose herself daydreaming, pretending her life was something other than the reality she lived with.

"I can see I'm disturbing you."

She took a quick breath, grounding herself in the present. "No, not really. I was just reading a book my cousin sent me from Vacherie. It wasn't something I'd expected," then she stopped. She'd almost begun to elaborate, telling him more about her life. What exactly was it about him that seemed to elicit confidences from her?

"You miss it. I mean your former home."

She frowned. "I miss things about it, Dr. Fallon. I'm sorry. I mean Jack. I miss, well, the security of understanding and knowing how my life would go forward."

He nodded, "I see. Its predictability."

His assessment left her feeling oddly dissatisfied. "That doesn't sound very good, does it?"

He shrugged, suddenly sitting in the chair across from her. She'd thought he was leaving, but now it seemed he was settling in for a conversation. He placed his bowler on the tabletop. "I don't know. I suppose the unknown can be unsettling."

"I've always felt—" then she stopped herself. What exactly was she about to say to him?

He leaned in a bit. "Please, you've always felt what exactly, Emma?"

"I've felt unsteady, I suppose, as though I did not belong anywhere." She laughed, "I know that must sound very silly to you."

"No, I understand completely. So, the predictability of your aunt's home was comforting in some respects."

"Just that I knew who I was or who I was supposed to be there. Here, well, I certainly have not found a footing."

He nodded with gravity, "And the book helps?"

She smiled. "Yes, in a way, it helps. I was happy when I would read it."

"Then, I won't keep you from it any longer. But I would ask one thing of you, Emma."

"One thing?"

"Yes, I'd like to take you to West End this Saturday."

She looked at him a little blankly. "West End? Whatever is that?"

In a fluid moment, he scooped up his hat, then added with a quick smile. "To my way of thinking, it's quite a magical place."

⚜

"But what is it exactly?"

Mattie Hart stirred her steaming cup of tea and looked very caught up in her own dreams of fancifulness. "West End? Really? I haven't been there for years. Benjamin and I spent a day there when we were first courting, but not since. Imagine that, and Dr. Fallon is taking you there. He must like you very much, Miss."

Emmeline let out an exasperated sound. She had tracked Mattie down to the kitchen and cornered her to obtain information, not to have to drag it out of her. She strummed her fingers on the white cotton tablecloth of the small table where she'd found Mattie enjoying an afternoon cup of tea. "Oh, I don't know about that. But I really would like—"

"Oh yes, Miss, my mother always said West End was a place for families or love birds. Would you like a cup of tea, Miss Emma?"

There it was again, Emma. Everyone had decided on this name for her, regardless of what she might want. "No, no, Mattie. Dr. Fallon and I are just friends, friendly acquaintances, nothing more. He's just being kind because, because of Mr. Nathaniel."

And then, at that moment, Mattie gave her an odd look, a bit sharp-eyed for the young servant that frankly Emmeline hadn't thought her capable of. "Yes, well, of course, Miss, if you say so."

"I do," she said a bit too quickly for her taste, but she felt defensive on the matter. "So, I really just wanted to know what it was, West End. Is it just a pretty part of the city?"

"Oh, yes, Miss, it's very pretty. There are gardens, lovely roses on trellises, as I remember."

"So, what do you do there, walk around?"

She nodded, "If you like, I was rather fond of the roller coaster or the carousel. That was my favorite. Benjamin would tease me about it."

She sat back in the chair, trying to piece together what was being said. "Roller coaster, carousel? What is this, some sort of park?"

"Oh yes, Miss, didn't I say? It's a lovely park with rides, restaurants, and boat trips if you like. And in the early evening, there is a concert where you could sit at a pavilion listening to it. And all sorts of sweets to eat, just everything Miss."

"Oh," she murmured, feeling her breath oddly taken away at the prospect. "It sounds lovely."

"Yes, Miss Emma, it truly is. But you'd better bring a coat. It gets particularly breezy near the lakefront. You'll be outside most of the day and a hat, of course."

"I always wear a hat," she murmured with distraction.

"Yes, of course, Miss," Mattie said, sipping her tea.

Emma nodded, "I think I'll have that tea now, Mattie, if you don't mind."

"Oh, of course, and I have some scones from this morning."

"That sounds wonderful," she said softly as Mattie got up to fill the tea kettle. But Emmeline's mind had been drawn elsewhere. Magic, he'd said. It certainly sounded like it might be.

⚜

It was this feeling going through her that she wasn't sure if she'd had before. It was a sensation of wild anticipation, greedy excitement, a sense of wonderment.

"I've never seen a place like this," she murmured as they strolled down a long, paved path filled with tents, vendors, amusements, and a massive Ferris wheel just down their path.

"Nothing like this in Vacherie?"

"Country fairs, but no, nothing like this." She pointed to an enormous architectural structure not far on the horizon, with tables and chairs beneath its pavilion and beyond the water with all manner of boats — rowboats, gondolas, and sailboats floating by.

"That's Mannessier's. I thought we'd have brunch there."

"It's a restaurant?"

"More of a confectionery, you know, pastries, coffee, ice cream. If that suits you?"

She felt like a little girl tantalized with possibilities. "It does," she answered, her eyes wandering eagerly across the diverse landscape.

"Do you like it, Emma?" he asked softly, squeezing her gloved hand that she had hooked within the crook of his arm.

But the environment distracted her so. She couldn't seem to take it all in. There were so many different types of people, children running and playing, and gardens with blooming flowers along divergent pathways. "It's wonderful. I'm just amazed."

Then he bent near her ear. "Would you like to ride the Ferris wheel?"

She glanced upward at its height, towering over the whole West End area. "I don't know," she murmured, feeling a giddiness fluttering in her stomach. "Maybe," she whispered.

⚜

Jack Fallon had picked her up in a hired carriage early that morning, and he'd told her the night before, while visiting Nathaniel, not to have breakfast. As they made their way out to the lakefront from which they took the long promenade of landscaped grounds, gardens, fountains, and other amusements up to the waterside, Jack was more than delighted by Emma's enthusiasm. It was as if something new and unguarded was opening up in her, something he was lucky enough to be privy to.

They sat outside of Mannessier's on the pavilion, having a late breakfast of pastries and coffee, and continuing to contemplate the great Ferris wheel and small roller coaster dominating the landscape.

"Your aunt never brought you to the city before?"

"No," she glanced back at him. Her eyes had been on the sailboats passing by the platform. "No, she took the other girls from time to time, but not me." She sipped her coffee, looking at him a bit sadly. "I suppose you think that's odd."

"No," he murmured. "Unfortunate, maybe, you seem to like it here. I mean, seem to get something out of it. Though I could be mistaken."

Her bright eyes clouded over just for a moment as she considered. "I don't know. I hadn't thought about it much. How do you know if you miss something if you've never seen it before?"

"True enough," he replied. "I do think that if you find a place you belong, you feel it on some level. Your spirit does in any case."

She smiled a bit at him, endearingly tipping her head. "Spirit? You mean religion?"

"Not exactly. In science, some call it magnetic fields, magnetism, or life vitality. Others call it a soul, spirit, the unseen life force beyond the flesh."

Her eyes were fixed on him, considering he thought, or perhaps simply trying to decipher what he was saying. "So, you think my magnetic self may simply know that I belong on that Ferris wheel?"

"Well, I was thinking more of you belonging in this city, but we can use the Ferris wheel as an example. That could be the case, if you feel instinctively drawn to it, like an unseen pull."

There was a flicker of amusement in her expression now. "A magnetic pull?"

"Indeed, Emma, a magnetic pull."

"I'm not sure I can say I'm feeling that."

"Really, no feeling at all?"

"Perhaps trepidation. It is awfully high."

"But I'll be right next to you to ensure you are perfectly safe."

✼

They did ride the Ferris wheel, ate pastries, and laughed quite a bit. And Emmeline knew without question that she was being courted. Although Jack Fallon did not behave like any other suitor that she'd ever come into contact with, though granted suitors for her had always been discouraged by her aunt. But there was something different here, something she frankly felt in the way he spoke, questioned her, and listened to her as though he were intently interested in what she had to say.

In some ways, it was flattering. In others, disquieting as though, well, he was definitely looking for something.

The day had already managed to stretch into afternoon when something curious did occur. They were strolling toward a restaurant within the West End Hotel for a late lunch, having just disembarked from The Camellia on a boat ride that toured Lake Pontchartrain. As much as she was enjoying herself, Emmeline felt more than a bit overwhelmed by all the activity. Just rallying her courage to get on the Ferris Wheel had been draining enough, although, in the end, she had to admit it had been one of her favorite rides. Beside her, Jack had remained jovial and unflustered by much of anything until, of course, an acquaintance of his intercepted them.

As they crossed a small bridge that led into a garden, a dark-haired man in a light gray suit addressed him from some yards away. "Jack, Jack Fallon," he called toward them.

Beside her, her companion didn't answer, just stopped abruptly as they were approached. Not far behind the man, who Emmeline observed seemed just slightly older than Jack, was a well-dressed woman in a fitted, teal-colored day dress who seemed content to wait behind.

Oddly, she felt a heaviness fall on the atmosphere around them that had been so delightfully pleasant only moments before. "Dr. Fallon," the man said, stopping directly in front of Jack.

Emmeline waited for introductions, but Jack took a moment before he replied. "Yes, Marcus, good to see you."

The smaller, dark-haired man eyed her curiously, making her feel slightly uncomfortable. "I must admit, Jack, I am surprised to find you here. You've been absent from the Society for some time, as has your good friend Dr. Lescale."

At the mention of her father, Emmeline straightened up a bit with surprise. "Yes, I've been occupied elsewhere, as has

Nathaniel." And then, after what seemed to be an age, Jack turned to her and said a bit dryly. "Marcus Becknell, may I present Emmeline Lescale."

The man in question looked upon her with evident interest. "Lescale?" he said pointedly.

"Yes, this is Nathaniel's daughter."

"I see," he said somewhat deliberately. And then he reached out, taking her hand and shaking it in a way that felt entirely awkward in the moment. "It is a great pleasure, Miss Lescale."

She smiled, glancing over to the woman who seemed inclined to still not approach any of them. "Ah, yes, my wife Monique, would you two care to join us for lunch?" he asked with a flourish that Emmeline had to admit felt insincere.

"No," Jack said pointedly. "Thank you, we have our own plans."

And then Marcus nodded, looking in a way that she could only describe as unsatisfied. "Of course, well, do give my regards to Nathaniel, and we hope to see you next month at The Society."

At that, Jack nodded, then took her arm abruptly and almost rudely began to move away from Mr. Becknell. She whispered to him as they walked away in virtual silence. "Was he a doctor too?"

"No," Jack answered flatly, "Marcus is an attorney."

"Oh," she said. "And this Society? What is it?" she asked, unable to quell her curiosity.

"Ah, it's called The Société du Magnétisme or rather, The Society of Magnetism."

Chapter 10

The Dinner Party

"Y ou look lovely, Miss."

Emmeline inspected the reflection in her bedroom's long rosewood cheval mirror. She wore a burgundy gown made of silk and velvet. The dress was actually one of only two evening dresses that she owned.

Originally, it had belonged to Genevieve La Maire, Aunt Adeleine's middle daughter. But the color had never quite suited her dark hair and more olive-toned complexion, so it was given to Emmeline as a bit of an afterthought.

"Do you really like it, Mattie?" She asked with a little uncertainty. She and Nathaniel were having dinner at Dr. Fallon's home this evening. It had been several weeks since Jack had taken her to West End on what she could only describe as a purely magical day. Even the strange interaction with Marcus Becknell had not marred this memory in Emmeline's mind. But after that extraordinary time, life on Esplanade Avenue had settled into somewhat of a routine with her slowly attending to domestic matters about the house or amusing herself with books and other hobbies. Several times a week, without fail, Jack showed up unannounced to see Nathaniel or escort her to a museum or a shop of interest in the city. And then, two days ago,

Dr. Fallon issued the invitation for dinner at Bienville Street. It had been somewhat unexpected, but Nathaniel had agreed. And now that the evening had finally arrived, she'd discovered that how she looked was suddenly very important to her.

The young maid smiled with genuine enthusiasm. "Oh yes, Miss, I'm sure Dr. Jack will agree."

She felt a flush of embarrassment. Was her intention that obvious? "Dr. Fallon has been very cordial to me since I arrived, Mattie, but that doesn't mean—"

"Oh no, Miss, I only meant he appreciates beauty. I've heard him say that over the years. And you are very beautiful, Miss, very much like your mother was, or so I can tell from pictures of her."

Emmeline, no, and she stopped herself, perhaps Emma tonight, nodded, continuing to inspect her appearance. She hadn't allowed herself to ponder the meaning of all this attention from Jack and where it could lead. In truth, Emmeline had no experience in that area and would not let her mind wander in that direction. Surely, she repeatedly reminded herself, he was just being kind to a dear friend's daughter. "Dr. Fallon said he would send a hackney to collect Dr. Lescale and I. Do you know if my father is ready?"

"No, Miss, Benjamin was attending to him. But I believe Mr. Nathaniel was having a bad spell today, but Benjamin gave him the medicine Dr. Jack had prescribed."

Emmel — or Emma as she was trying on tonight — looked up a bit disgruntled. This was the best-kept secret in the house, Mr. Nathaniel's bad spells. In all her time here, she had yet to witness exactly what one of her father's "spells" actually looked like. Mattie and Benjamin had been deliberately opaque about the matter and also seemed adept at running interference so that she could not witness any of his symptoms. In truth, the situation was beginning to irritate her immensely. After all, she was his daughter. At least that was the pretense upon which she'd been brought here in the first place.

"Mattie," she said a bit sternly. "I would very much like it if you would explain exactly what you mean by one of Dr. Lescale's spells."

Mattie's bright blue eyes widened a bit. "Um, Miss, it's no matter. Dr. Jack has things under control."

"Dr. Jack does?" she said a bit sharply.

"Yes, Miss, and he did tell us to be discreet to protect Mr. Nathaniel's privacy."

"Protect it? From me?"

There was undeniably a protracted hesitation. "Maybe you should speak to Dr. Jack about this, Miss," she said in a low, nearly inaudible voice that told Emma she would dearly like the questioning to just stop.

She frowned. This was spoiling her previously buoyant mood. "Yes, perhaps I will. Can you please check if Mr. Nathaniel is ready?"

"Oh yes, Miss," and then she exited quickly. Clearly, her inquiries had made Mattie a bit uncomfortable. But she wasn't fond of secrets, particularly when they were being kept from her. So, she would uncover what was being hidden and soon.

⚜

It was dusk by the time they arrived at Jack Fallon's house. Her father, Nathaniel, was quiet, fully cordial to her but clearly distracted by thoughts or concerns that he did not seem inclined to share. But, of course, in her short time in New Orleans, she found that he did not seem inclined to share much.

"Have you visited Dr. Fallon often?" she inquired on their ride in the hackney to Bienville Street.

"From time to time."

"So, you have known him for some duration?"

"Yes," he answered, not elaborating, his dark brown eyes focusing on her as if he had noticed her for the first time. There was a chill in the air tonight, so her father wore a long overcoat over his suit, and Emma wore a gray woolen cape trimmed in black velvet that her Aunt Adeleine had given her.

"Did my mother know him?" she asked, not at all sure why, except that she felt nervous about tonight, exceedingly nervous for some inexplicable reason.

His eyes narrowed a bit. Of course, he truly didn't like speaking of her mother. She'd found this on many occasions when she brought her up. "No, Lizette had died before Jack came to live here."

She stared out the window of the carriage. The black, cast-iron gas streetlamps illuminated the streets, which gave everything an eerie glow on this foggy night. "And so, I was long gone by then," she murmured nearly to herself.

"Were you very unhappy in Vacherie, Emma?"

She turned back to him with surprise. His voice was direct, not muffled and discordant as it usually seemed when he spoke to her. "Not unhappy, not particularly happy either. You know it wasn't actually as if I belonged there."

His expression in the semidarkness was unreadable. "Yes, well, it is a difficult thing in life to find a place where you actually belong. Did they mistreat you, my child?"

She frowned. "Extraordinary question to ask now, don't you think? But to put your mind at rest, no, not in essentials."

Nathaniel responded somewhat wearily. "Yes, then I would have to say you have fared rather well given what could have been."

❀

The house seemed larger than her father's home, but she couldn't be sure. Curiously, the stucco and brick structure was completely attached to the building next to it. However, it did appear to go up several stories with a prominent set of balconies decorated by black wrought iron work. The driver drove them through a long, arching carriageway entrance along the side of the structure back into a spacious courtyard, much larger than

Nathaniel's, illuminated by several gas light fixtures. Almost immediately, Jack Fallon walked out of the house to greet them and help her and Nathaniel from the hackney. As he took her gloved hand, he whispered in her ear. "I am so glad you are here, Emma," and then, after paying the driver, he took her arm and escorted her inside.

The evening itself moved along at a fluid pace. After a lovely dinner downstairs, where several servants attended them, Jack brought them to a parlor overlooking Bienville Street, where the front of the house was located.

Here, there was a fireplace that was lit, as well as a brocade recamier sofa and several velvet bergère armchairs. Although Jack had kept her engaged in light conversation for most of the evening, she found her father had been more subdued during the meal, only responsive when Jack directly addressed him. Once in the parlor, he'd settled into a chair near one of the French doors and sipped a brandy while she and Jack drifted nearer to the fireplace. She whispered to him as he handed her a glass filled with port. "I'd like to speak to you about Nathaniel."

He smiled, not seeming terribly surprised at her request, "Of course," he answered smoothly, directly addressing her father. "Would you mind very much if I gave Emma a quick tour of the house, Nathaniel?"

Nathaniel looked up at him again with that peculiar, disconnected expression that Emma had been witnessing with him all evening. "Yes, of course, I'll just rest here. I've been feeling strangely tired all day."

Jack smiled at him, patting his shoulder, then heading to the doorway, waiting for Emma to precede him. "Just this way," he murmured.

⚜

Although this had not been her intent, Jack did seem focused on guiding her through the house. As they passed through various doors, Jack pointed out different rooms, several large bedrooms, a small study, and the hallway beyond the stairwell. They descended an outside staircase, passing through a lovely loggia and then into the courtyard. And that was where they stopped near a small fountain and an outdoor cast-iron table and chairs.

"Are you too cold?"

She shook her head, just acknowledging that she'd left her cape inside, but the burgundy dress had long sleeves, so she did not feel the chill of the November night as much as she might. "Do you garden?" she asked, a little surprised, staring at a small plot on the side of the courtyard filled with green plants.

"Some," he answered, not elaborating but pulling out a chair for her. "Did I mention how beautiful you look tonight, Emma?"

She smiled, feeling a slight warming of her cheeks. "Thank you, dinner was lovely, Jack. Everything has been—" her voice drifted off as she tried to figure out just how to get into what she wanted to discuss.

He sat across from her, looking a bit more intense than he had in the preceding moment. "Best to launch into it, I suppose."

She frowned a bit, "Launch into it?"

He tapped his fingers absently on the table in front of them. "Quite honestly, Emma, you are going to find me a rather direct fellow. I don't like to waste time. You wanted to discuss something."

She straightened up. This she did find strange. She'd come from a place where subtleties and non-direct communication were served as a main course all day long. "Yes," she began, "it seems that Nathaniel has been experiencing some sort of spells, if you will, that Mattie and Benjamin seem inclined to try to keep from me. But which I understand that you seem aware of and perhaps are treating him for."

He leaned back in his chair, eying her intently. "Well, it didn't take you long to ferret out this," he said softly.

She clasped her hands together on the white table, taking a deep breath to steady herself. "Mattie and Benjamin aren't very adept at concealment."

He looked down, continuing to strum his fingers. "Yes, Nathaniel is ill," he said with little emotion. He glanced up, seeming to focus on something a bit beyond her. "Do you like the house, Emma?"

She shifted a bit in the hard chair, feeling somewhat perplexed by the sudden change in subject. "The house? Yes, it's very nice, but what—" then he looked at her directly, and she stopped mid-sentence.

"He is ill, deteriorating, Emma. It is a curious malady, seems to be centered in the brain."

"Mental?" she whispered.

"Of a sort," he said gravely.

"Is this—" she said haltingly, unsure if she really wanted the answer, "is this why I was brought here?"

And then he looked at her with significant focus as though turning over some great matter in his mind. "Why don't you take some of your port? It might help just now."

She picked up the glass on the table and took two substantial burning sips that went down rather roughly. But she didn't care. Her mind was spinning, trying desperately to grasp what she was being told. "I don't understand, Jack."

He spoke slowly, deliberately, as though he was giving significant thought to the words he chose. "I owe Nathaniel so much, Emma, my life here, my work, and other things you know nothing about. The truth is that I won't see him locked up in some barbaric mental facility as his faculties fade." He expelled a somewhat tortured breath, she thought, but then again, perhaps she was being dramatic. "You see, I want to bring him here. I can set up rooms for him in the back garçonnière where I can assure that he is taken care of properly."

Her heart had picked up its beat in mounting anxiety. "Is it really that bad? Institutions? I just don't understand."

"Yes, I can see that, Emma. The fact is that if Nathaniel becomes incompetent, which I fear his condition is rapidly progressing to, then he will be unable to make his own decisions legally. His next of kinship will make those decisions for him."

"You mean me?"

And then he frowned, and a distant awareness caused her stomach to flip a bit. "Possibly, but to be blunt, as a woman, a conservatorship may be granted elsewhere — to a male relative who could—" then he stopped.

"Have him committed?" she finished for him. "I-I don't know how that could be prevented," she whispered.

"Easily," he stated, taking a quick sip of his brandy and just as smoothly returning it to the table. "If you had a husband, he legally would make those decisions."

The world seemed to spin a bit as a heavy blanket of silence felt as though it were thrown over them, muffling out all thought, all coherence. "Husband?" she echoed his word.

"Yes, Emma," he stated very calmly. "To be blunt, I want you to marry me so that you and Nathaniel can live here, and I can see that he is cared for."

His words, startling to her sensibilities, felt like cold, icy water splashed across her mind. *Used* was the description that seemed to emerge from the ashes of what she'd formerly considered quite a lovely evening. "So, you had me brought here?"

His gaze was direct, unflinching. "I encouraged it."

"Does my father understand this?"

"No, not really."

"You manipulated him."

"It's for his own good, Emma."

She stood up. It was such a strange moment. It felt distinctly as though all the air had flown out of her lungs. "I'm sure some legal papers could be drawn up, Dr. Fallon, giving you some conservatorship over my father without including the necessity of marrying me."

"I've explored that," he said softly, watching her closely. "That could be challenged."

"Why would that happen?"

"All I can say, Emma, is that your father was involved in important research that many would like to get their hands on. Powerful, dangerous knowledge that in some respects could be responsible for his present condition." The face of Marcus Becknell flew through her mind, and her stomach sank at the realization.

"So, you had me ripped from the life I knew?"

He eyed her unflinchingly. "You were needed." This blunt, succinct way he spoke to her felt very cold.

"Well, how very romantic! How could I possibly resist?" She snapped out, then began to walk quickly away from all of this madness. But Jack was on his feet, grabbing her arm firmly and compelling her to face him.

"I understand that this is quite a bit to take in."

Her heart was racing. She was angry, in fact, consumed by it. The deception, all of it, incensed her to the core. And beyond that, she felt so foolish to believe he might have genuine feelings for her. "Do you really think so, Jack? Do you really expect me to marry a man I barely know to help protect a father who has ostensibly abandoned me all my life?"

His face hardened. "It certainly does seem unfair. But I can give you a good life, perhaps even make you happy, Emma."

She roughly yanked her arm away from him. "I very much doubt that, Dr. Fallon," she nearly hissed as she headed back to the house in a blind rage.

Chapter 11

Between

Emma, no Emmeline, she suddenly insisted to no one in particular but perhaps herself, did not know where she was going. She was just flying forward with emotion. A pawn in someone else's game, that was all she had ever been. She did not feel overwrought about her father's illness. He was a stranger to her — a father who had chosen to be a stranger. And this, Jack — Dr. Fallon— had swept into her life pretending. There were tears, hot tears of rage pouring down her face, pretending that he would be a friend to her, someone who might actually care, while really only plotting to use her for his own devices.

Blindly, she tore up the outdoor wooden staircase, nearly tripping on her burgundy skirt. She didn't know if he was following her. Her mind was reeling from the impact and explosion of so much bottled-up emotion. She was hurt, deeply hurt from so many things that she had pushed down for so long — pushed them down in a way that made her believe foolishly that they did not exist. She thought she was removed, detached, pragmatic, but what she felt like now was pathetic, pathetic to believe even just for a moment that she had consequence to someone, to anyone. All of this just felt like pain ripping through her heart and dizziness sweeping through her. As she reached the landing, her head was swirling.

It crossed her mind that she was slipping into one of her sick-headache episodes, but the headaches never came on exactly like this, so quickly. She grabbed hold of the outside railing along the balcony. Her vision was spotty, swirling with colors. And then a very icy fear gripped her. Was she ill? Was something terrible happening to her?

Her knees were giving way, as she slumped down until a powerful pair of hands went around her waist, abruptly pulling her up.

"Now, now, hold yourself together," she heard him say, a familiar voice. But the darkness wouldn't stay away as she collapsed and was swept up into waiting arms.

❦

"Here, sip this." Her eyes fluttered open briefly as a glass was brought to her lips. The liquid itself burned her throat when she tried to swallow. Aggressively pushing it away, "What is it?"

"Brandy," he said softly, taking the glass and placing it on a nearby table. So difficult to move, her head was still spinning with dizziness, but she did try to sit up.

Placing his hands on her shoulders, he softly but firmly pushed her back into a reclining position. She glanced around, instantly recognizing the large parlor as the one upstairs on Bienville Street.

"Where is Nathaniel?" she asked, looking to Jack, who was standing over her. Her vision had begun to clear, and she realized that he'd changed clothing and wore a different suit — dark gray, no vest, shirt untucked. But surely there hadn't been time to change.

Around her, everything felt confused. The fire had gone out, and there were odd subtle changes about the room, paintings not quite the same, a chair or two different and shifted in position. Her head now began to ache. What was this?

She sat up deliberately, now looking around critically. This made no sense. But for the two of them, the room was empty.

"Where is Nathaniel?" she demanded sharply.

Jack was looking at her calmly, too calmly, she thought, after the exchange they'd had downstairs in the courtyard. And then she suddenly noticed his hair wasn't quite right either. Impossibly, it seemed longer. His beard was clipped a bit differently. She rubbed her temples. She surely must be losing her mind.

"Emma, it is important you tell me the last thing you remember."

"What?" she expelled sharply. "My name is Emmeline, not Emma, Jack." Now, she remembered how angry she was at him, how outraged. "You were there, in the courtyard, telling me you wanted to marry me so that you could look after my father."

There was a hesitation in his eyes, then she heard a perceptible sigh come from him. "I see," picking up the glass again. "It might be good to take a few more sips of brandy."

She put her feet on the floor, looking around again with confusion. Her head was still spinning. "Why has everything changed? Have I lost my senses?"

He sat down slowly in a bergere chair adjacent to the sofa. "Of course not, but all of this has been done very badly I'm afraid."

Staring up at him, a fresh wave of upset overtook her at the night's events. "I don't understand what's happening here, nor why you deceived me this way."

He frowned. "Yes, that too was very badly done. I'm sorry, Emma. You have to understand I was impulsive in many ways in my younger days."

"Your younger days?" she repeated, stumbling over the words and looking at him with confusion. "What in the heavens does that mean?"

He held out the glass toward her. "Perhaps a little more, Emma."

Frowning, she took the glass and then tentatively sipped it. Again, the intense burn in her throat, then something else nearly immediately following — a sudden sleepiness overtaking her.

Rising from his chair, Jack walked to her and then pushed her back on the sofa, lifting her legs so that she was reclining.

"What is this?" she whispered.

"This, my love, is for the best," then she felt him softly kiss her lips before she fell asleep.

✣

She awoke to find herself on a bed, a canopied bed with an ivory satin cover in a room that she did not recognize. As her vision focused, she saw Jack standing near the doorway. Jack dressed in the earlier suit, the black one he'd worn this evening. She squeezed her eyes shut. And then it crossed her mind that perhaps her father wasn't the only one losing his faculties.

"Emma," he said softly, patting her hand. "Are you all right?"

Slowly opening her eyes again, Jack was now sitting next to her on the bed, looking genuinely concerned. She thought to say Emmeline again, but it seemed a minor point at the moment. "I suppose I really have no idea," she nearly whispered.

"You collapsed on the stairs, and I brought you here." He squeezed her hand. "I truly didn't mean to upset you so much. I should have waited, given things more time."

"I saw—" she hesitated at how nonsensical this would sound. "I saw you in the parlor, Jack, but different, in different clothes. The way you looked was odd. But you were talking to me."

His eyes reflected something, perhaps a bit of surprise, but still, he said, "Maybe a dream, Emma. You were unconscious for a time."

She looked away from him in confusion. "Maybe," she murmured. "Could you get us a carriage?" she said quickly. "I think I'd like to go home now."

He stood up from the bed and walked to the door, which he abruptly closed. Startled, she sat up, finding that her head was still dizzy. "What are you doing?"

His face suddenly looked stern or should she rather say determined. He spoke slowly, "Yes, of course, you can go home, but not until we get a few things straightened out."

She crossed her arms protectively in front of her, feeling a chill creep over her. "I think I have had quite enough for one night, Dr. Fallon."

And that was strange because it made him smile, smile as though he were oddly pleased. "You see, Emma, there were things I knew before I met you. I knew that you would be my wife. I knew that you were extraordinary, and I knew you were a traveler."

She felt oddly concerned, nervous a bit, by this change in his demeanor. He seemed different somehow. Dare she say threatening? She brought her legs over the edge of the bed and stood up with effort. There was still that grogginess from — then she remembered the dream. He'd given her the brandy and then the overwhelming sleepiness.

"He drugged me. I mean, you did in the dream."

He frowned a bit, "That would make sense. Too much, too soon, but then it can't be helped."

She moved, edging away from him. She wasn't sure why, except that she did not know what to think or what any of this could mean.

She felt a piece of furniture behind her, a wardrobe she thought she remembered seeing, but he continued to move toward her. "Stop now, right where you are, Jack Fallon," she said firmly. "I demand you let me return home this very instant."

Again, the smile, "So it's home now, Emma, not Nathaniel's house."

"Stop it. How dare you use my own words against me."

He did stop but stood just in front of her, where he could easily reach out and touch her. "I am not trying to frighten you."

It was true. She was breathing heavily. She was afraid, afraid of so many things. "I don't understand what you're saying, Jack. How could you know things about me before we met? What do you mean, a traveler?"

He didn't touch her, but he leaned closer, putting his hand on the cypress wardrobe above her head. He was looking at her strangely, making her face feel flushed and her heart race with uncertainty inside her chest.

"The problem is we simply haven't had enough time, Emma. We need to slow things down a bit."

"I don't know what you mean," she said in a heavy whisper, and then he showed her exactly what he meant as he moved closer to her, then put his lips to hers. It was a shock, the contact, so unexpected. Then the warm feeling pooled through her as his arms went firmly around her body. She must resist, but it was so hypnotic. Her mind sort of shut off as he deepened the kiss. Then that mad swirl and a high-pitched sound in her ears as though some storm swirled around her, perhaps within her, followed quickly again by the blackness.

Chapter 12

Traveling

The voices, all around her, inside her head, were mounting in volume. *"There is no place for her."*

She was running, running through the darkness, yet there was muffled light around her. It hurt. All these thoughts, all these words ripped through her in pain. She saw the black water of the Mississippi. Maybe she should have done it then and ended all this unnatural torment. She stopped, leaning against the cold stone wall of the tunnel. The ground beneath her feet was brick-laid like the roads outside. It was confusing. She couldn't quite remember where she was, then saw the dull glow ahead. Slowly moving forward, she recognized that this was the carriageway on the side of his house, where their hackney had traveled through to the courtyard. Her limbs felt sluggish, weighted like lead. But as she looked forward toward the glowing lights, she could see people gathered in the courtyard.

Without thought, she moved toward them, but then suddenly a pair of arms slipped around her waist, yanking her backward.

"Best not to engage unless you know what you're dealing with. All sorts pop out around here." Jack whispered harshly into her hair. And then he firmly dragged her into a nearby doorway against the house wall on the side of the carriageway. Rather roughly, he pulled her inside, closing the door behind them.

"Quiet," he whispered to her. From what she could see, his face looked a bit clammy to her in the semidarkness. "Hopefully, they'll move on."

She backed against a shelf in what appeared to be some sort of storage room. "What is this?"

He waited a moment more, then grabbed her hand and opened another small door. "Come on. I'll explain inside."

"Jack," she began, but he wasn't stopping, just aggressively pulling her through a corridor.

"It's safer upstairs, but we can't use the outside staircase."

She was completely disoriented, having no idea where they were going. All the house was dimly lit, not at all as she remembered earlier, but perhaps it was late. He led her to an inner stairwell situated along a brick wall. The stairs they climbed were small and very steep.

"Come on," he repeated insistently, propelling her in front of him, nearly pushing her up the staircase.

The incline ahead dizzied her. "I don't want to fall."

"I've got you. Don't worry," he rasped.

She could feel his hands on her back, her skirt, guiding her, but quickly as though there was some impending threat. Finally, she reached the landing, but there was no banister to grab hold of. But then his arm was supporting her, touching her clearly wherever he felt was expedient.

When had this happened, this familiarity? But then she remembered the kiss, the intimacy, warmth, and desire she had never experienced before. But had that even really occurred?

He had her hand now and was pulling her again. And suddenly, they were back in the parlor. She stopped in the center of the room as Jack moved quickly to close the wooden shutters over the French doors. Glancing at the fireplace, she saw there was no fire now. And oddly, it looked quite cold, as if it had not been lit at all.

"Where is Nathaniel?" she asked, remembering now having asked that before, when she asked the other Jack. But then, that couldn't have been real.

He finished locking the shutters, turning back to her. "He's not here, Emma," he said simply as though that were a sufficient response.

"Yes, I can see that," she spat out with a degree of unbridled aggravation, or perhaps it was hysteria at this point. "Where is he? And why are we hiding? Isn't that what we're doing?"

"To a degree, I suppose," his voice sounded a bit out of breath. But then, of course, they had practically run only moments before across the length of the house.

"To a degree? What the devil does that mean?" she nearly exploded.

And then he turned to her, moving more closely. "All right, first, your father is resting, just where we left him when we went to the courtyard to speak. And when we return, it will be for him as though no time has passed."

"When we return? Return from where?"

He just stood there, infuriatingly staring at her intently without answering as though debating his response. Then finally, after what seemed an age, he spoke, "Well, I call this place *In Medio* or rather the *Between* if you prefer."

Emma stood in the dimly lit parlor in James Fallon's New Orleans townhouse, wondering with a degree of panic if her father's dear friend had completely lost his wits.

"What did you say?" she asked, momentarily taking stock of his appearance. His tie was hanging loosely, undone. His shirt was unbuttoned several buttons, vest, as well, completely undone. And then, somewhat abruptly, he removed his suit jacket and tossed it onto a nearby chair. His face was reddish, and there were spots of perspiration mottling his shirt in various places as though he had greatly exerted himself.

He breathed deeply as he repeated, "I said that I call this the *Between*."

"Between?" she echoed. "What are you referring to? We are simply in your house."

He moved closer to her and said softly. "Emma, surely you can feel the difference."

"Difference?" she muttered rapidly. "Other than Nathaniel is nowhere to be seen, and you are hiding from a group of people collecting in your courtyard."

"Well, it is close, admittedly very close to where we were before, but there are differences, important ones." He said with emphasis.

"You know, you're talking nonsense, Dr. Fallon. I have to tell you that I have had quite enough of all of this. You've been acting quite alarmingly all evening, from insisting I marry you in the courtyard because Nathaniel is having some sort of mental breakdown, to later when—" she stopped herself realizing, perhaps best not to bring that up.

"When I kissed you."

She wrapped her arms around herself, expecting to pull her wrap in more closely, but realizing with disorientation that she didn't have it. She'd removed it earlier. It was just her in her burgundy-colored dress that she'd picked out, especially for this evening, which had now evolved into something unintelligible. And sometime during this internal dialog, he'd moved toward her. In fact, he was standing just in front of her now.

"Did you like it when I kissed you, Emma?"

She stepped back instinctively. "That wasn't the point at all."

He frowned. "I can see that, all business. What a pity, so you think I'm a madman?"

"Well, I sincerely hope not, Dr. Fallon. But all of this — whatever you are trying to convince me of — causes me to suspect as much." She didn't sound afraid or betray the shakiness she felt rising inside her. It was a technique she'd employed while living with her aunt. Often feeling utterly bereft of allies, putting up a good facade was essential. But now, staring down Dr. Jack Fallon, she had no idea if it was working.

"Would you care for a brandy?" he said unexpectedly. She frowned, remembering the brandy the other Jack had given her that she now suspected was laced with some sort of sleeping draught. "No, no brandy," she murmured.

"Then more port, perhaps. I suspect you never had adequate time to finish the first one."

She probably shouldn't drink more. There was wine with dinner, but then again, with the insane swirl of events, her nerves were exploding with agitation — a little calming might just help. "All right," and then she added impulsively. "You aren't going to put anything in it, are you?"

He smiled briefly, and she wondered why he would find that amusing. "No, I need you alert," he said softly, handing her the glass. "Come and sit next to me so I can tell you a story."

❦

He was surprised, certainly pleased that she was holding up as well as she was. She did look a little flushed, her cheeks abnormally pink, but given the strain of the last several minutes, that was to be expected.

And, of course, Emma was upset, clearly with him. That, too, was to be expected. Granted, he should have taken his time with things. Honestly, due to his arrogance, he now realized in retrospect that he hadn't expected her to resist the idea of marrying him. After all, he was established, had his own house, and was a fairly handsome man in his way, or so female acquaintances had told him. And given her situation, Emma's prospects for a good marriage were not substantial.

But then again, she had said that she would never marry. That emphatic statement by her had been a surprise and concerned him. But, due to his own conceit, unquestionably, he had refused to take it too seriously. After all, marriage to him wouldn't be like marriage to anyone else. His error, or perhaps safer to say one of his errors, was that he hadn't taken the proper amount of time to try to change her mind — impatience on his part.

So, he acted, did ostensibly the only thing he could think of — bought himself more time.

Emma was seated on one end of the recamier sofa, holding her drink but not sipping it. Her eyes were cast downward as though she had no desire to meet his direct gaze. He supposed he deserved that.

He walked across the parlor to the fireplace. The fire here was not lit as it had been in the other place. He couldn't have predicted if it would be. There were always variations depending on how close or how far one landed.

"Did you know that your father is keenly interested in the Hermetic Sciences, particularly alchemy?" He said, placing his drink on the mantle.

Her eyes rose to meet his at the question. In this particular lighting, they appeared green, green and wide. "I know next to nothing about Nathaniel."

The stark pronouncement struck him distastefully. It had to be acknowledged that Nathaniel Lescale had been unfair with his daughter, more than unfair, selfish in his dealings with her. "Yes, well, when I came here to live in New Orleans, I discovered that Dr. Lescale held many private interests beyond those I had already known — the physical sciences, chemistry. In addition, he'd deeply studied the esoteric sciences — chiefly the works of Paracelsus, Roger Bacon, John Dee, and Franz Mesmer, just to name a few. In fact, rather than just studying them, I would have to say he was steeped in them."

She placed her drink on the chestnut gueridon table beside her because, as he'd noticed only moments before, her hand had begun to tremble ever so slightly. "What does any of this mean?"

"Please bear with me, Emma. Nathaniel had traveled a bit after your mother's death. These travels and studying with what I could only describe as adepts in Egypt, the Middle East, and

Europe sparked this interest. So, when I entered his sphere, he took me on as a sort of apprentice to his work."

"Work?" she questioned. "What kind of work are you talking about?"

"All kinds, transmutation, magnetism, alchemical, astral projection and," then he hesitated. "A particular kind of traveling."

"What does that mean, traveling?"

He frowned a bit at the inquiry, unsure how his answer would be received. He sat down right next to her on the sofa. "I very much wanted you to see this house, Emma," he abruptly took her hand in his. "It's an extraordinary place. That is why I acquired it, actually just three, well, nearly four years ago. You see, this city is filled with powerful energy points, bands, I like to call them. It makes this sort of traveling much easier."

"Traveling again," she said with a tad of exasperation. "What can you possibly mean?"

And then he said softly, although she couldn't help but detect steel in his voice. "Traveling, my dear Emma, through planes of existence, dimensions if you will."

Chapter 13

Ghosts

There were always moments that she had found in her life — peculiar moments when it felt as though the earth itself were shifting beneath her feet, where the world she once knew, had held firm footing upon, was no longer there for her — no longer substantial.

It had happened once at Belle Coeur when she was merely five years old. Before that, she had existed rather happily inside that lovely cocoon nature provides for very young children, a lack of awareness that creates an illusion of security. It is a tragic thing when it is shattered too early. For her, she was five, accidentally overhearing a conversation between Aunt Adelaine and one of her cousins, the youngest, Pauline.

"Isn't it lovely having Emmeline living with us? She's like another sister."

"Oh no, my dear, never think that. That girl is less than all of you. It is only through our charity that she remains — abandoned by her derelict father. Out of respect for my parents, I give her a roof over her head."

"But Aunt Lissette?"

"Spirited girl and not quite right in the head. Let us hope our poor little Emmeline did not inherit that disposition."

It's a sad day indeed when that protective structure collapses. Before this, Emmeline had believed she was loved and foolishly thought she was being treated as an equal. If there were slights or disparagements, they did not enter her immature awareness. Only later, when suspicion and paranoia were allowed to creep into her Eden-like existence, was everything reflected upon and analyzed at length. What a disturbing and sad day, as was this one unfolding before her.

She didn't speak, didn't respond to his proclamation. She knew better than that. He had just declared to her with all appearance of genuineness that he and her father had taken to traveling through dimensions, planes of existence. She didn't have to be of great formal education to know that what he was speaking of was indeed insanity.

And in conjunction with all of this was, of course, the stark reality that she was indeed alone in a room under the control of a madman.

He had walked across the parlor as though in some state of agitation, right near the fireplace. "Did you hear me, Emma?" he said somewhat forcibly.

She glanced beside him. Black, somewhat rusty fire irons strewn across the hearth would make excellent weapons.

"Yes," she said, forcing herself to speak calmly. "It is difficult for me to absorb. That is all."

He looked at her strangely then, unreadable, as though in contemplation. She glanced around the room. On his desk, there was some sort of obelisk made of white stone. She could also reach this more quickly, but not as easily as the "Fire iron," he said flatly. "Definitely a better choice for a woman of your stature."

Something that felt physical dropped down into the pit of her stomach, cold fear, perhaps.

"What?" she managed shakily. "What did you say?"

"I said you should choose the fire iron as your weapon. To smash me somewhere, I would assume. And I must say that your Aunt Adelaine sounds like an awfully cold-hearted bitch."

Her mouth was dry, and the ground, yes, the ground beneath her feet, felt as though it had undeniably shifted. She stood up, although she was sure the wooden floor might give way at any moment. "You, you know my thoughts," she stammered.

His face was eerily stoic, hard. It frightened her and left her with the distinct impression that he was losing patience. "Here, it is easier. Forms are not as impermeable as they are where we usually live. You see, thoughts are actually energy forms. If you focus, it is much easier to intercept their import." He picked up his brandy glass from the mantle where he'd hastily placed it moments before and took a sip as though considering for a moment. "It's also why they seem so physical here. The ones you saw outside. You see, they don't have physical bodies as we do. But their belief that they do is so strong that it manifests."

She shook her head. "What are you talking about? The people I saw in your courtyard?"

"They're not people, Emma. They're lost spirits that haven't found their way to the next plane of existence. They're ghosts."

She took in a sharp breath. "This is madness."

"Yes, I can see why you'd think so. But the truth is that if you managed to dispatch me, somehow, you wouldn't get on here very well by yourself."

"Here again? What are you saying, Jack, that we've actually traveled somewhere else?"

He laughed shortly. "Yes, what do you think all this is about, Emma? We've traveled to another dimension."

It came in a wave, the dizziness sweeping past her, through her. She felt his quick movement, his arms going round her, beneath her, sweeping her off her feet. She didn't slip into the darkness, but her vision was mottled with swirling colors, phantoms of shapes separating from their physical forms floating in rapid distortion in front of her eyes.

He was carrying her, carrying her into another room. "I don't understand this. Why would you do this?"

He didn't answer, and she didn't feel his arms about her. The dizziness enveloped her as she closed her eyes, squeezing them shut.

⚜

"Lizette, Lizette," she heard a name being called, not hers, her mother's. Opening her eyes slowly, she found she was lying in a bed with a man standing beside her holding her hand, trying to rouse her. But it wasn't Jack, not Jack at all, but instead, a much younger version of her father.

Nathaniel's eyes widened as she sat up. She tried to take it in. It was the same bedroom she'd been in with Jack earlier when he'd kissed her, but he was nowhere to be seen now.

"Lizette," Nathaniel Lescale said with emotion as he squeezed her hand. She pulled it away from him abruptly. "No, I'm not Lizette. I'm Emmeline."

"Emmeline?" he whispered, seeming confused. This was confounding. He was undeniably a younger him, hair not so gray, body not so thin, and his face not nearly as lined with age.

"I, I am sorry, my dear. You look so much like her. Of course, there are differences, but I thought that might be a side effect of the translation. There are always anomalies and aberrations in a transference," he rambled on.

She backed away from him, feeling deeply uncomfortable at his presence just now. "Where is Jack?" she demanded.

"Jack? Back in the laboratory at my house. How did you come to be here, my dear? I have not seen you since you were a child."

She backed away, flinging her feet around the other side of the canopied bed and down on the wooden floor. Again, the dizziness swept through her like a storm, but she forced herself to stand. "I was with Jack. This is his house."

"His house?" the man questioned with confusion. "He lives in a boarding house on Conti Street. He has no house."

"I see," she said shakily, again wondering if, somewhere along the way, she'd simply tumbled into her own delusion of some sort.

"I was trying to reach your mother, Emma. Something has gone wrong, but you look so much like her, my dear. Tell me, are you happy, Emma?"

His eyes were looking at her intently, almost with desperation. It was too much, so she simply backed away until the door was behind her. Once she could feel the ceramic knob in her hand, she yanked it open and launched herself out, blindly heading through the house. She had no idea where she was going until she reached a set of French glass doors, which she quickly opened, only to be greeted by the cold night air.

The staircase again, she lifted her burgundy skirt and began to head down when she was suddenly jolted, caught by a pair of strong masculine hands. Fully expecting to see Jack Fallon, she was spun around aggressively.

Her breath seemed to rush out of her lungs, and her voice felt trapped in her throat. She should scream, but she was incapable, struck completely mute by fear.

It was a man, but one that she did not recognize. He was dressed entirely in dark formal evening garb and a top hat. But his face was pale, horribly, unnaturally pale, nearly white. And as she looked further down, she saw across his throat, right through his shirt collar, a huge, garish, gaping slash, as though his throat had been slit, and blood had soaked the front of his dress shirt.

She yanked backward, finally finding her voice and screaming stridently as she tumbled down the wooden steps.

Chapter 14

Adventurers

Her mother was smiling. She wore that long blue dress she remembered from her dream. The two of them were outside at night, her parents, in a courtyard, but not the one on Bienville Street. This was somewhere else.

This courtyard was well illuminated under a star-filled night sky and landscaped beautifully, with flowers blooming everywhere. Lizette held out her arms, and the man who embraced her was Nathaniel, her father, but younger, different, his face beaming, filled with hope, she thought with distraction.

Then they began to dance, silently waltzing across the brick-laid patio — the only sound being Lizette's enchanting laughter piercing the stillness of the night.

*

When she opened her eyes, she was in the parlor again, lying on the sofa. Jack had a chair pulled up beside her. Her shoe on one foot was off, and he was wrapping a heavy bandage over her stocking.

Instinctively, she started to pull away, but he placed a hand on her leg, stopping her movement. "Be still," he said calmly, intently focused on his work. "Your foot was twisted badly beneath you when I found you."

"Found me?"

He looked up into her eyes. "Yes, Emma, I found you at the bottom of the stairs. You'd taken a nasty fall."

She straightened up on the couch in alarm. "I remember. I remember a man grabbing me. He wore evening clothes but looked like someone had cut his throat. He grimaced, tucking the ends of the bandage so that it would not come out. "That should give you some support. It didn't feel to me as though anything was broken. But you have to be careful here, Emma. You can be hurt just as easily as you can be hurt anywhere else."

She looked at him intently. "Who was that man, Jack?"

His eyes focused somewhat solemnly on hers. "From your description, I imagine it was George Battiste. He was a businessman, lived in this place in the 1700s. Evidently, from what I can gather, he fell on hard times, borrowed some money, and failed to repay it."

"You mean he was murdered," she murmured.

"Yes, well, most ghosts don't have a particularly peaceful ending to their lives."

"He's a ghost? But I felt his hands on me."

"Yes," he said flatly, "as I told you, where we are enables them to achieve a more physical manifestation. You seem to have a strong gift for traveling, Emma. I lost track of you after our last conversation."

"I saw Nathaniel."

"I see," he said quietly.

"He seemed to be looking for my mother."

"Yes, one of Nathaniel's primary goals was to reconnect with your mother somehow."

"And did he?"

He shrugged, standing up and walking away. "You'd have to ask Nathaniel that, I'm afraid. All of this did take a particular toll on him."

"This traveling, as you call it?" she said slowly.

"You know Emma. You must try to be calm. This high emotion is making your excursions unpredictable. To remain safe here, you must exact a measure of control."

"How can I hope to control something when I have no clue how or why it's happening?"

"Yes, well, I assumed you'd stick by me when I brought you here. You know, the last thing I intended was for you to get hurt." And then he looked at her rather grimly. "I think perhaps that we should go back."

She stared back at him a little blankly. A thousand images crowded through her head at once. There was George Battiste, the businessman, with his throat cut. There was her father calling her Lizette, evidently traveling from some past point, even before Jack Fallon had set foot in this house. There was her dream about what she was now convinced was an older Jack. But now was the question of whether it was indeed a dream or some *traveling episode*, as Jack termed it.

And then there was the kiss, something she hadn't allowed herself to even ponder during this rapid chaos of events. There was that kiss that was powerfully romantic and sensual at the same moment, and the sensation only moments ago of feeling his hand on her leg as he bandaged her ankle. It was undeniable. There was a powerful current between them — a draw that she'd resisted. She'd known it when they'd first met that night at the riverboat landing, and she knew it now.

Go back, he'd said. Going back to what, she wondered — organizing her father's Esplanade Avenue house, trying to get flowers to grow in a courtyard that had clearly already seen its last bloom of life.

And that was the crux of it, the crux of it all at this moment. She felt alive, alive in a way she hadn't felt since she was a little girl, and her aunt had mercilessly burst her serenity. There was possibility now. Even if all of this was truly madness, there was wild possibility.

She straightened up on the sofa, bringing her feet down to the floor, and allowing her burgundy satin skirt to swing down as well, brushing down around the top of her black velvet slippers. There was a slight twinge as the ankle hit the floor, but certainly not unbearable. She looked Jack Fallon straight in the eyes with steel in her back. "No," she said clearly.

He stared back at her with what registered as a bit of astonishment on his face. "No?" he repeated with emphasis, although as a distinct question.

"No," she said again. "There is so much here that I do not understand. And I would like to take the time to understand it."

The expression that crossed his face was not particularly unreadable. A smile flickered on his lips, and a sparkle touched his eyes, giving her the distinct impression that they had crossed an invisible line somewhere. That the ground beneath their feet had indeed somehow shifted in the way that it does, and they had now both become, for lack of a better description, adventurers.

⚜

He was surprised, confounded, and somewhat amazed. There was so much that he clearly didn't know about Emma Lescale. But there were a few things that he'd gleaned from his recent exposure to her, and of course, the time he'd spent with her future self.

She had an independent nature. She didn't like stagnating, and she was intrigued and compelled by the new experience. However, she might try to hide these inclinations; they were indeed core to her character. These were aspects of her that he'd hoped to gain leverage through. That was why he'd brought her here — to a bold new landscape where he could ostensibly seduce her literally and figuratively. "So, do I understand you correctly, Emma? You do not want to go back?"

She frowned a bit, or at least he might call it a frown, rather a singular pursing of her lips. She was at war with herself, battling that self that she felt was expected of her through her circumstances and the culture of the time. Battling with this and that other self, the authentic self that he so hoped he could reach and unleash. That was the Emma he wanted, in fact, at the moment, wanted quite badly.

He moved closer to her because he could, and there was nothing to stop him. He sat down next to her on the sofa and quite possessively took her hand in his. It was cool, but he could feel the blood racing beneath the skin. He was attuned to such things, and then again, there was the energy — the sacred fire, as the alchemists termed it. He could feel it when he touched her, when he felt her thoughts, that flow between them, the elemental draw that had so much potential. "You don't have to guard your thoughts with me," he said softly. "Tell me purely what you think."

"I'm intrigued, enticed, I suppose," she murmured quietly. He grasped the hand more strongly, and now there was a warmth, blood rushing unconsciously toward the contact.

"There are so many things that I could show you here," he said a bit thickly. He had to get hold of himself, or he would become overcome by the powerful emotions and sensations she was eliciting in him.

"I feel," then she hesitated, and he squeezed her hand to encourage her to continue. "All of this feels familiar, strangely."

"Yes, walls, separations that usually exist become more permeable here — time, dimensions, realities are easier to reach through, to touch."

"I-I don't know Jack. Even you seem as though someone I've known for a long time, although my mind tells me we just met."

He took her other hand, holding them both together on his lap. "Feelings, senses are more important here, Emma. Your mind can confuse you."

He spoke with distraction. So much was happening. There was the powerful attraction of touching her skin. He knew it would be strong, but he had no idea. It was beginning to block out his power to reason.

Her breathing had picked up, her heartbeat, the flush on her skin, around her face, her throat. He shouldn't rush things no matter how much he dearly wanted to. "So, you're staying for a bit," he said.

"Seems so," she answered.

He was trying to think, puzzle out the best course of things while still holding her hands, wondering which way to go next.

"Jack," she said softly.

"Yes, Emma."

"Do you really want to marry me?"

He turned to her, looking intently because he had no choice. "Of course I do."

"Because of my father, that is the reason."

He looked at her, a bit confused. Oh yes, that was how he'd made the case. "No, not just that, I'm in love with you," he stated quite flatly.

Her eyes widened with genuine surprise. "How can that be? We've just met."

He thought to explain but decided not to. Instead, he let her hands go and gently put his palms on the sides of her face, pulling her closer and then covering her lips with his.

Chapter 15

Return

She breathed in deeply. There was cool air sweeping all around her. She pulled the bedspread more tightly in, sheets and blankets up to her chin.

"Sorry, Miss, I can close the window again if you like."

Her eyes fluttered open with difficulty. Such a powerful lethargy clung to her. It took every effort for her not to relax and fall back into a slumber. She glanced around through watery, blurry vision. She was back in her room, her bedroom in her father's house on Esplanade Avenue. Pulling the covers down a bit, indeed, she was dressed in her nightgown — one she had no memory of putting on last night.

"Are you all right, Miss? You look very peaked," Mattie proclaimed with concern as she bent over the bed and peered at Emma. Mattie had freckles. Strange, she hadn't noticed it before. But then again, she'd never had the young red-haired maid in such proximity.

"What time is it?" she whispered in a somewhat croaky voice.

"Going on three o'clock in the afternoon, Miss Emma. You slept through breakfast and lunch." She pulled herself up in the bed, feeling a quick rush of light-headedness that did not go unnoticed by Mattie. "Would you like me to fetch Dr. Jack for you, Miss?"

"What? No, I'm all right, just tired."

"Well, the doctor did say you might be that way after all the events of last night." Mattie had straightened up and looked at her with a peculiar smile.

"Events?" she echoed with confusion.

Her mind worked hard to piece together what she remembered the night before. The last thing, and it was the very last thing, was sitting in the parlor of Jack's house, Dr. Fallon. And he'd just begun to kiss her, then nothing, nothing at all.

"Yes, Miss, you and the Doctor. He said that you were engaged."

The words impacted like a huge rock hitting her directly in the face. She abruptly sat fully up in bed. "He said that!"

She grinned back at her. "Yes, Miss, he seemed very happy about it. He is quite a sought-after bachelor, and you two only knowing each other for such a short time. But I don't blame you. Every girl who meets him sets her cap for Dr. Fallon, but he's taken a shine to no one else like you, Miss."

"I didn't set my cap for him," she mumbled in confusion.

The smile dimmed a bit. "Oh no, Miss, it's clear how taken he is with you, and, of course, he loves old Dr. Lescale like he was his father."

Her spine suddenly stiffened in determination. "Mattie, I need to get dressed," Emma said brusquely, her head spinning from the odd rush of events. Had she accepted him? She remembered a discussion in the courtyard. But how could she have accepted him and not even remembered? "Could you help me, please? I do feel a bit shaky."

"Oh yes, Miss, Dr. Fallon said he would call this afternoon. Maybe he could look at you."

She grimaced. How dare he tell everyone that they are engaged. She didn't remember that, not even a glimmer of it. "I'm sure that won't be necessary."

✤

She sat outside in the courtyard, wrapped in a light rose-colored shawl that had been Pauline's. Her gray muslin dress didn't seem warm enough to drive away the chill that clung to her. She hadn't seen Nathaniel. Mattie said he'd spent the day barricaded in the study, working on some project. Wasn't that odd, she thought? If there indeed had been some sort of engagement announced, wouldn't he have waited to take the time to congratulate her, speak to her about it in some capacity? But then again, Jack had said his mind was slipping. That was when he'd made his proposal, such as it was. She did remember Jack saying that he'd wanted to marry her so that he could look after her father. But later, he'd later told her he was in love with her. Hadn't he? So strange how that particular recollection had become foggy, intangible.

And besides, how could that be? He scarcely knew her, and she— Well, how did she truly feel about him? She actually had no idea.

Emma distractedly nibbled on a biscuit that Mattie had insisted she eat and sipped a cup of hot tea.

And there was still the fatigue. Her mind was having trouble grasping the wild, convoluted crush of events from the night before. What had been real? And the rest, if it wasn't, was it part of some dream, some strange illusion?

She heard one of the doors from the house as Jack Fallon strode out slowly into the courtyard. He wore a gray suit this morning. Perfectly matched her muslin dress, she thought grimly.

He didn't say anything, just pulled out a wrought iron chair across from her and sat down at the small round patio table. "How are you?" he said rather calmly, with little expression on his face.

"Tired," she murmured. "And quite confused."

He nodded, intensely focusing on her. "Well, don't fight it. Sometimes it's an effect, the body adjusting."

"Adjusting?"

"Yes, Emma," he said tentatively, "adjusting to the traveling."

She took in a deep breath. "So, that was real? I mean, it all feels a bit confusing now."

He looked at her intently as though carefully considering what she was saying. "Yes, Emma, all of that was real," he said rather deliberately.

She lifted the tea to her lips. It was a delicate little cup, china, decorated with silvery flowers. Just holding it made her think of her mother. And she wondered with distraction if, indeed, Lissette had sipped from the same cup. Gingerly, she placed it back in its saucer.

"I thought it might have been a dream or imagination. You know, I really don't remember coming home last night."

"You don't?" he said, seeming a bit surprised. "Well, traveling can sometimes jump ahead in the timeline. It may come back to you, or it may not."

"And I don't remember," she hesitated, "agreeing to marry you."

He was unpredictable, this man, at times appearing quite stoic and at others reflecting deep emotions. This time was the latter. She could see the impact of what she'd said on him. Clearly, he'd thought the matter was settled. And the fact that it wasn't presented quite the dilemma.

"Ahh—" he said with some amount of concern. "Well, that does create a problem."

"Does it?" she asked.

He paused for a moment, then leaned across the table, taking her hand in his. "So, then I'll have to ask again. With all my heart, Emma, I'm asking you to be my wife."

His hand was warm on hers, and she knew that this, this proposal of sorts that apparently was now happening undeniably, probably wasn't wise. All of it was occurring too quickly, although as she remembered it, Pauline's engagement and nuptials had occurred rather rapidly, all within a few months. But for her, this was so fast, and the truth was she knew very little about this man except that he was extraordinary and clearly led an unusual life. And she also knew, without understanding why, that when he said he loved her, she believed him. But with all of this, there was something about him that unquestionably felt a bit dangerous.

"Jack," she began softly, unsure what to say. "You must know that this is happening so very quickly."

"I do, Emma, but sometimes life defies our expectations, and we simply have to grab hold."

Her throat was dry, and the breeze was still chilling her. And she couldn't be sure why she did, except perhaps because she had done so before, but she did say yes.

⚜

There is a particular chemistry involved in human contact. When one touches the skin of another, an actual chemical reaction occurs. Energy can travel for good or ill within the contact. It was alchemical, a notion that many people might dismiss, and, of course, the more intimate the contact, the more powerful the reaction that takes place.

There was a woman, a widow he'd met at a boarding house where he lived when he'd first moved to New Orleans and became a medical student. She owned the house, and through comments, attention, and unsolicited contact in passing, it became more than clear that she was interested in a liaison.

"Have you slept with her?"

"What?"

He was taken aback by the directness of Nathaniel Lescale's inquiries. After all, he'd been raised a gentleman and felt decorum insisted that he not be too forthcoming.

"Nathaniel, that's not something I—"

"Enough of that boy, have you?"

He frowned. He'd only been in the city just over a month and hadn't yet become accustomed to the man's abrasive manner. "No, I haven't."

"But you've touched her, kissed her, seen her undressed?"

"To a degree, what exactly does that have to do with—"

Nathaniel sat behind his desk, flipping through a rather old book entitled *Theatrum Chemicum Britannicum* by Elias Ashmole. "Here," he pointed to a rather intricate illustration. "You see the diagram. Triangle pointing up —masculine, triangle pointing down —feminine, masculine, and feminine forces in the universe. When merged, they create the six-pointed star, a very powerful esoteric symbol. Sexual intercourse isn't just physical, my boy. It's alchemical. It ties the mind, body, and spirit and can create a powerful reaction — creates spiritual energy. Do you see?"

His mind was swirling a bit. Nathaniel had begun to speak to him about his alchemical research, but so far, it had been limited. "So, that sounds like a positive occurrence," he mumbled, still put off by the old man prying into his personal business.

Then Lescale eyed him strangely, "It's a powerful thing and therefore dangerous as well. If the lady in question is a proper spiritual match for you, powerful bonds and energy can be created for your benefit. But if she is not, the bonds created can be used to cause great damage and drain energy. Such intricate connections should not be taken casually or lightly. They can forever alter and derail the course of one's existence."

He frowned with a bit of irritation. "So, you are saying a liaison with Mrs. Godfrey might alter the course of my existence?"

"She's already draining your energy, my boy."

"Draining my energy?"

"Yes, I can see it, the odd aura patterns around you," he declared emphatically while staring intently at Jack in a very unsettling way. "There are ceremonies we can do to weaken these bonds you've foolishly created."

He laughed uncomfortably, "You make her sound evil."

The old man, as he was always fondly apt to call him, shook his head dismissively. "Not evil, all spirits go through a stage where they can drain others to try to further their own development. Of course, it never works — something they need to learn. But it can be quite damaging to those they prey on."

"So, just kissing the woman?"

"Kissing, touching, any skin contact, seeing her nude, all of that can be used. It might be best for you to move in here for a while until we get this sorted out. Make no mistake, my boy. With the right person, such intimacy can be a revelation."

And so, not long after, he had left young Mrs. Godfrey's boarding house and moved in for a while with Nathaniel Lescale and spent time, much time, studying and learning to view his world in different terms.

Still Between

Jack kissed Emma Lescale, passionately kissed her. He had basically propelled her into a nearby but alien dimension, actually more easily than he had expected. In many ways, she was very adept at this or would be in the future, as he'd found through his contact with her future self. She had gifts, and she was, as he'd known from their first meeting, and the first time he'd touched her, extremely well-suited to him. Now the trick would be convincing her of that. And without question, they'd gotten off to a rocky start.

It had been a mistake to introduce the idea of marriage with the goal of taking care of her father. Foolishly, he'd believed that might appeal to her pragmatic mind, but then again, pragmatism clearly wasn't the soul of her. It was simply the facade she used to protect her inner self.

So, he'd told her he was in love with her, direct, jarring perhaps. And he'd kissed her, easily able to transfer energy within the contact — a soothing, calming energy was his goal. But perhaps he'd overdone, not yet at ease with how receptive and susceptible she was to him. Relaxing too much, she'd collapsed in his arms.

There was a feeling of floating, relaxing of her mind, body, and skin. Her eyes were closed, but she was more than aware of her surroundings — voices passing in and out of her consciousness.

"You shouldn't worry. Whatever is meant to be will happen."
"That seems an odd position for a doctor."
"I've come a long way from truly believing I can control everything. That simply isn't the nature of existence."
"But what if I lose this baby like the other ones?"
"Then we hold onto each other and move on. I love you, Emma. Always remember that."

It was painful hearing the emotions and beautiful at the same time as they rippled around in a wave.

Everything felt fluid, moving, evolving. Slowly, she opened her eyes, feeling arms around her, strong, consistent arms. She looked into Jack's face. He was holding her tightly, looking around them sternly, then she glanced over his shoulder and screamed maniacally.

He turned around, frowning impatiently. "Yes, well, I suppose it was only a matter of time."

"What are they?" she rasped, clinging to him fearfully. What she saw seemed to be strange bugs, huge, black and orange with scurrying antennae, scampering around the wall — two impossibly huge ones.

"Parasites," he murmured. "Looking for something to eat."

Chapter 16

The Engagement

The next few days became a bit of a blur. Memory of the time at Jack Fallon's house on Bienville Street seemed to be vacillating between trying to return in vague snatches of foggy images and retreating, just as an elusive stretch beyond her grasp. It was frustrating and concerning to her at the same time. What had happened that night? And why had it incited her to accept the marriage proposal of a man she barely knew?

Of course, she'd thought to back out once she reflected on things. Her acceptance felt impetuous on some level, certainly not well-considered. She must reverse herself. It seemed the only sane course of action. And she'd decided to do just that once he'd left the house. In fact, that was what she intended the very next morning when he arrived after breakfast. But then he had brought his mother's engagement ring, a lovely piece of jewelry with sapphires surrounded by diamonds. It caught her off guard, and she tried to broach the subject, but he'd easily drawn her in another direction. And in addition, there was always her father or Mattie or Benjamin with them at all times, no private moment for her to explain the situation to him, though how exactly she would explain she had no concrete notion. All of this was making it increasingly awkward for her to beg off.

And in truth, beyond all of these circumstances, it was him as well, Jack. He had this way, his very manner, of making things so much easier, making her feel as though marrying him was the best and only decision she could make. And he truly seemed to care about her, genuinely.

That, on top of everything, made it all so confusing. Did she honestly want to marry this man? Did she? Her father had insisted Mattie accompany her to get a new dress, for which he would pay, for the ceremony, the ceremony two days away in a small chapel off of Royal Street. Everything seemed to be moving so quickly that there wasn't even really time to invite her relatives from Belle Coeur. And regarding that, she wasn't at all sure if she wanted to. The problem was that she was indecisive, not sure of much of anything.

So, amid all this indecisiveness, she had decisively decided to pay Dr. Fallon a visit at his home on Bienville Street. That was what she would do — talk to him directly, honestly. She would secure a hackney and settle this matter once and for all.

Between

His hand wrapped around her waist, and he pulled her jarringly to the other side of the parlor. She was horrified, literally, couldn't take her eyes off them — two, the size of small children, thin, wiry, insect-like things scuttling around the fireplace. Their heads, misshapen bug-like heads, orange and black, were covered in strange multiple eyes and odd pincer-type jaws snapping where their mouths should be. Truly, they were monsters in the worst sense of the word.

"Great God, Jack, how did they get in?"

"They live here. I'd imagine. We're in between, you know, another dimension. All manner of things live near us that we don't know about. Can feel sometimes, but never actually see."

"But they're in your house," she hissed, not being able to remotely understand what he was rambling on about.

He hooked his arm around her, nearly dragging her into the hallway and through another door, closing it firmly behind them. She glanced around. It was a bedroom. She remembered that she had been here before. In fact, Jack had kissed her here before.

She took a step backward. "I want to go home now."

He gave an audible sigh, "You certainly are changeable. We need to wait a while. Clearly, these parasites sensed some vulnerability, or they wouldn't be here. Might be the ghosts outside. They're always bleeding energy."

"Bleeding energy, what does that even mean?"

He focused on her, frowning as though he suddenly realized how nonsensical what he was saying must sound. "I'm sorry. This must be a bit overwhelming to you."

It did take a slight moment for the understatement of his description to filter in. "Overwhelming?" she gasped. "Yes, yes, a bit."

He ran his hand through his disheveled hair and motioned to the bed. "Why don't you sit down, and I'll try to explain a bit more?"

She glanced around nervously, eyes landing squarely on the bed and recognizing for perhaps the first time that she was in a bedroom alone with this man, but then again, it wasn't the first time. But she did quickly recall there were substantially large monsters outside, so perhaps decorum could be safely brushed aside just in this instance. She sat down, looking at him expectantly. "The bugs?" she prodded.

"Yes, well, from what I have discovered, they are parasites of spiritual energy. They feed off what we carelessly spill."

"Spill?"

"Yes, in varying ways, we wound our spirits, and instead of losing blood, we lose something much more valuable, spiritual energy."

"You said the ghosts."

He nodded in agreement. "Yes, yes, a person by virtue of not crossing over after death to the next plane is forcing their spirit into an unnatural existence."

"Damaging it?" she murmured.

"Exactly," smiling a bit at how quickly she was catching on. "So, they are constantly losing energy. Some even become spiritual vampires."

"Vampires?" she repeated dubiously, wondering with distraction what sort of a gothic dime novel she had stumbled into.

"Yes, those who drain energy from the living."

She stood up abruptly. This was truly too much, vampires indeed! "Dr. Fallon, you can't possibly expect me to accept all of this fancifulness as truth."

"And yet you did see the parasites in my parlor."

"It's just not possible," she whispered as much to herself as anyone.

"You'd be amazed to know just how much is possible."

❧

Jack Fallon was working quickly, in fact, very quickly, because he must. He was clearing out the garçonnière for occupation by Mattie and Benjamin downstairs and the whole upper floor as a suite of rooms for Nathaniel. It was his plan to relocate them all to his home as expeditiously as possible once he and Emma were married. Married this Saturday — he dearly hoped, strumming his fingers on the desk, wondering if indeed everything would go off as smoothly as he planned or if, and there was a pronounced sinking feeling in his stomach area, or if, instead, things would just get more complicated.

He stood up and paced the length of the room. He'd arranged to take a week off from his duties at the hospitals and his practice so that he and Emma could go away together.

He'd acquired rooms at a lovely inn on the Gulf Coast — precisely what they needed, some privacy, some time for things to settle. All of this he'd planned, that was if she indeed went through with marrying him at all.

Again, he walked the length of the room. He sensed it, of course, every time he saw her, a growing unease. He was more than sure all the memories from that night hadn't returned. In fact, he'd focused intently to envelop all of them with a vague, hazy quality. So, if she'd managed to retrieve them, there would have been questions, so many questions. He did know without a doubt that they would be married, provided he didn't inadvertently derail his future. But it was true that he'd met his future wife in this house on more than one occasion. But getting there, making the correct moves, well, that was another matter.

As an unexpected awareness crept in, he crossed to the front window overlooking the street below. He watched with some curiosity as a carriage stopped in front of his house. Immediately, he recognized Emma as she stepped onto the pavement and then paid the driver. He smiled, a bit surprised. Well, no chaperon, clearly propriety was not uppermost in her thoughts. Fleetingly, he considered that perhaps he could compromise her, then marriage might seem like a necessity. After all, he'd never considered himself the most scrupulous of men, particularly when it came to getting what he wanted.

Still Between

She frowned, suddenly struck by the absurdity of this situation. "And why did you bring me here again, Jack?"

The question seemed to take him by surprise. "Why? Yes, to give me time."

"Time for what again?"

"To convince you to marry me," he said a bit awkwardly.

"Really, with parasites in the parlor and ghosts in the courtyard?"

"Yes, well, I suppose I didn't really consider that aspect of things."

"I should say not. I mean, with all of this. How could I possibly refuse?"

He grinned, "But I know you, Emma. You do like a challenge."

"What does that mean? How do you know that about me?"

He'd moved closer, standing right in front of her. "When you first came to the city to live with your father, you were thinking of striking out on your own, becoming a governess or something of that nature."

Her eyes widened, "What! How could you possibly know that?"

"Well, your thoughts were easy for me to pick up on, some of them, at any rate."

"My thoughts! You've been reading my thoughts all this time?"

"Some are easier than others. But it is true, you seem rather accessible to me."

"Dr. Fallon!" she said hotly, standing up and finding herself much closer to him than she intended. "Do you realize what an invasion that is? If I actually believe that it is possible."

He smiled softly, placing his hands on her shoulders. "You might want to calm down, Emma. The parasites, you know, are drawn by negative energy."

"Negative? What do you—"

"Sadness, anger, upset, all negative, darling."

"Don't call me that, darling. Why are you smiling?"

"Sorry, it's just that I get a strong feeling now that you are going to marry me."

❦

She was nervous. That he could sense immediately. He thought perhaps that it was probably not wise to meet her alone, but his curiosity got the better of him.

He escorted her out to the courtyard. Instead of allowing him to take her shawl, she requested they come outside for some fresh air. It was late afternoon, and he'd already taken care of his rounds for the day. He sat down at the cast-iron table and waited, waiting for her to initiate the conversation, which she did not. Instead, she sat across from him, not meeting his eyes, and fiddling nervously with the ends of her shawl.

"Emma," he said, perhaps a bit too sharply. Her eyes shot up at his tone, meeting his gaze. "What on earth is the matter?"

Her chin trembled a bit — so clearly nervous, working up the courage to speak. "Jack, I'm sorry. This is so difficult. You see, I feel as though I've misled you. I—"

He stood up abruptly, taking her hands in his. "Emma, you really should come inside. Your hands feel chilled." She began to pull them away, but he firmly maintained contact. He tugged at her, pulling her to her feet and into a close embrace. Contact was important, essential. It would help things. He touched her hair, stroking it lightly, holding her firmly. He whispered, "Don't worry. Everything will be fine." And then he began softly rubbing her arms with his hands, trying to soothe her. The energy he sent out was designed to make her relax and, yes, to a degree, be complacent about things. It wasn't the noblest thing he could do. But it was important that they be married. So, he used all the tools at his disposal.

She breathed in deeply, "I barely know you, Jack Fallon. How on earth could I have consented to marry you?"

He stopped for a moment, pulling back a bit and giving her an odd quizzical look. "But Emma," he said softly. "You have agreed already, in fact, twice."

She looked at him strangely, trying to remember. He could see the broken flashes through her mind — his parlor, at night, but so much was happening. Then, he deliberately pulled her closer. "Not yet," he murmured.

Jack held her again against him, so closely in his arms. In the plainest of terms, he was weaving a spell. All he had to do was manage her through the next few days. And once they were married, then he would set things straight. It wasn't really fair to Emma to handle things like this. But the truth was that he needed her and couldn't risk her slipping through his fingers.

"Everything will be fine," he said soothingly in a lulling tone, and all of his senses felt everything snap into place. This would hold, at least for a time.

Chapter 17

Just a Dream

"I have a daughter."

Jack looked up from his book. He'd been deep in the study of a volume by John Dee. It was now just about a year since he'd moved into Nathaniel's house on Esplanade Avenue. His medical studies at Tulane were progressing well, as well as his tutelage into the esoteric and occult fields with Nathaniel. It was late in the evening, and they were indulging in brandy while Jack took the opportunity to peruse some of Nathaniel's books. But as it was, he was sure he'd misheard. "What was that again?"

Nathaniel was looking at Jack very intensely. "I said I have a daughter. She is about six or seven years younger than you, Jack."

Slowly closing the book and more than a bit perplexed, "A daughter, Nathaniel? How can it be that you haven't mentioned this until now?"

The old man sighed and took a sip from his glass. "I have to say that I was too ashamed."

Jack frowned, realizing for perhaps the first time that there were facets to his mentor that he had no clue about. He put the oversized book that he'd held in his lap aside, now focusing with curiosity on the man seated in front of him. "Where is she, your daughter?"

"Living in Vacherie with relatives of my late wife, Lizette, they took her in when she died. It happened not long after the baby was born, and I felt ill-equipped — no, that's not really true. I felt I'd be poison to the child." He seemed to be looking beyond Jack as he spoke with such a cold voice, nearly haunted. "When she died, she took everything you know. I wasn't sure if I'd be able to go on. And I knew without a doubt I'd be no good to Emma."

"Emma?" Jack repeated."

"Yes, Emmeline, but she called her Emma. Lizette had picked out that name for a girl before the child was born."

"And you haven't seen her since?"

He shook his head. "No, but I did send letters, but with no response."

Jack continued to stare at him with confusion. It felt unquestionably as though there was something more here. "Why are you telling me this now, Nathaniel?" He said slowly.

"Lizette told me last night that the girl needs you."

"Lizette?" He stumbled across the name, "Your wife?"

"Yes, Jack, she still speaks to me, in dreams mostly. She said you need to contact the girl."

"Contact? How exactly should I —"

"I don't know precisely how Jack. But you should find a way."

✢

She wore a traveling outfit, dark brown wool edged in brown satin piping. It was a two-piece construction with a fitted, flattering bodice flowing into a tastefully arranged bustle and a long tulip skirt. Nathaniel had purchased it, but she was intent on being practical in the choice, wearing short lace-up boots under the long tapered outfit. It was to be a small affair. She assumed they would be married at the Esplanade Avenue House, but Jack insisted on the ceremony at a chapel, followed by an elaborate breakfast at her father's house. The planning of the nuptials, she felt oddly distanced from. She had not thought to invite anyone from her aunt's family. Of course, she would send them a letter about it later, to her aunt and Pauline. She wondered distantly if her cousin would be hurt not to be invited. But again, that thought was distant, disconnected, not touching her emotions as none of her thoughts seemed to. After brunch, she and Dr. Fallon would leave, leave on their bridal trip. Thus, the wedding outfit doubled as her going-away attire.

She stopped brushing her long blonde hair. She was sitting in her room at the vanity table, staring at her reflection in the mirror. Slowly, she let the brush lower down to the table's surface. It was a large brush with a ceramic back decorated with delicate purple flowers. It had been Pauline's. Many of her things were items she collected because someone no longer wanted or had use for them. And she'd been grateful for them, treasured them in some respect.

She stared at her reflection. Yes, she and Dr. Fallon would leave on their trip, not far, he'd said, a place near the water. She'd never believed she'd wanted to get married, but here she was, the night before her wedding. She thought about Jack, Jack Fallon, but when she did, she felt a curious peacefulness cascade across her mind. He told her that he would take care of her.

Did she need someone to take care of her? She was not a child. He'd given her a lovely bracelet made of dark blue stones — lapis lazuli, he'd told her. It was quite lovely and had belonged to no one before, just her.

She breathed deeply. All these ramblings in her mind felt curiously detached, devoid of connection. She was sleepy. Tomorrow was a wedding day, rather, her wedding day. But then again, she considered that maybe all of this wasn't real at all, maybe just a dream.

Between

She didn't know what had come over her, maybe frustration, maybe disbelief, or maybe just a sudden surge of insanity. But something broke inside. She bundled up her burgundy skirts so that she might move quickly, circumventing Jack Fallon, throwing open the door to the bedroom, and bolting out quickly.

"Emma," she heard his powerful voice yelling after her, but she didn't care. She rushed through the hallway that connected to the outside stairwell. Before anyone or anything could reach her, she was on the steps, careening downward toward the courtyard. Dizziness swept through her as did a powerful chill, but she plunged further onward. She had no idea where she was headed, just that she needed, needed to breathe, perhaps.

In panic and confusion, the one thing that flew through her mind was home, home and familiarity, and once the dizziness began to clear, astonishingly she recognized it. She was standing in the middle of the great foyer at Belle Coeur just in front of the grand staircase.

She tried to draw in breath, but it was difficult. It wasn't from the great exertion of tearing down the corridor in Jack Fallon's house and down that outside staircase, but because of something else, something insidious, something external.

"Emma," she whirled around in the semidarkness because everything here was cast in thick shadows.

He reached through the blackness, putting his hands on her arms. "This is a bad idea, Emma."

Pulling away from him aggressively, again she felt the struggle to pull air into her lungs. "Where are we?"

"You know," he said softly.

So strange, she heard his voice, but it also seemed distant, disconnected. "I don't. It seems like Belle Coeur, but not really."

"It's a shadow," he whispered. "I really believe this is too much for you to absorb now. Take my hand. It's best we go."

She reached out for the hand he'd extended, but hers seemed to pass right through his like it was a phantom. Somewhere in the darkness, there was a hiss. And her eyes could scarcely focus on the things moving down the staircase, dark, slithering things heading toward them. "Oh God, what are they?"

"Concentrate on me, Emma. Concretely focus on returning. This place is treacherous to you now."

She closed her eyes and, with all attention, held onto the image of returning to Jack's house in her mind.

✤

Her head was spinning as her feet finally touched the ground beneath the staircase. The outside seemed quiet, but with a deep steadying breath, she headed to the carriageway tunnel that led to the street. She didn't hear Jack anymore, nowhere any longer.

Emma continued to move. Maybe she could just head home to her father's house. She hadn't seen much of him this evening. Perhaps he was already there.

The tunnel was dark, although she could see streetlamps illuminated well beyond it, lamps peering dusky light through the fog. Her head continued to swim with the dizziness that was becoming a hallmark of the evening. She glanced back again to the courtyard, but it was empty this time. No one was there. Then she turned around back toward the street and stopped with a jolt. Because suddenly now there was someone, a man standing in the shadows directly in front of her, barring her way.

Instinctively, she stepped backward, then felt her foot twist badly within her burgundy skirt. The sharp pain of it caused her to sink down onto the stone pathway. It was the injury from before, the one Jack had attended to. But now it throbbed painfully as she looked up into the shadowed light. The man was standing over her now, then quickly crouched down beside her, his hands suddenly on her arms.

Glancing up, she took a sharp breath as she quickly identified him. It was Jack again, truly, but not at all the one she'd left in the bedroom. So very different — so much younger, maybe just into his early twenties.

"What have you done?" He murmured. And with the strength in his hands, he pulled her up to her feet.

"I-I," she rambled in disbelief. It was true. This one was utterly clean-shaven, with no beard or mustache. She reached out, touching the smooth side of his face. "How can this be?" She said shakily.

He pulled her next to him, supporting her as he walked her slowly back into the courtyard. "Why are you out here alone, Emma?" he asked.

"I was running," she said breathlessly, her mind whirling dangerously with confusion.

"Running from what?" The younger Jack asked.

"I-I'm not sure now," she said shakily.

He hesitated a moment, then replied softly, "I see," muttering a bit, though not seeming as surprised as perhaps he should have been. Silently, he led her to sit on a wooden bench on the side of the garden. She eased onto it slowly with his help, pain still shooting through her ankle.

As he sat down beside her, she noticed Jack, younger Jack, was dressed in a simple white shirt and black pants, not the suits he usually wore. "And this house, Emma, is it yours?"

More than a bit befuddled, she murmured, "No, it's yours, Jack."

He glanced around as though he'd begun to examine it critically. "I see," he said softly, "and why were you running from it?"

She began to answer, then stopped, unsure what she should say. "I – I don't know. I got overwhelmed. So much was happening so quickly."

He patted her hand gently. "You know, however it seems, I would never do anything to upset you. I care for you deeply."

"You wanted to marry me."

He laughed aloud, "And that's why you needed to run?"

"I-I don't like losing control of things, and everything now feels madly out of control."

He squeezed her hand with a bit of a grin. "What a pity. Losing control is one of my favorite things to do."

She took a sharp breath and wondered, not for the first time this evening, if she was losing her faculties. "But that's madness."

He smiled again, amused at her, an expression that she had seen more than once on his older counterpart's face. "Living is madness, Emma. It's truly all how you look at it."

She felt exhausted, deflated. She had no idea what to do now — escape, go back, stay here, collapse — all choices seemed valid and nonsensical at the same time. "This is just too much," she whispered.

He patted her hand lightly, and it did calm her. Oddly, physical contact with all the varying variations of Jack Fallon always seemed to calm her and, to a degree, soothe her ragged soul.

Slowly, she rose to her feet. "I need to find a way back now to puzzle all of this out somehow."

He was standing next to her in the semidarkness. "What did you use to do when you were upset at your aunt's house?"

She looked at him with confusion, given her very recent experience there. "Why do you think I was upset at Belle Coeur?"

There was no smile. He seemed quite grave. "I would see you there at times, alone in a room upstairs."

"The attic room," she whispered.

"Yes, the attic room," he said. "You seemed very upset, and then you would focus on something, and that would calm you down."

His face seemed so young, but it was the same eyes. Why did he always look at her so intensely, as if he were looking for something in her?

"I remember," she said. "I remember thinking about another life. That I was living another life where I was free and happy."

Again, he squeezed her hand that he held in his own. "Maybe here is where that life could be."

She smiled sadly. She wasn't one to tantalize herself with false hope. "I don't know."

He nodded thoughtfully, "Very well. I believe you should take the stairs back to the second floor and clear your mind as you do. I will do my best to get you back where you belong."

"How is that even possible?" She said with real curiosity.

"Energy, focus, and a susceptible landscape, trust me, Emma. I would never do anything to harm you."

She frowned, feeling the sharp pain in her ankle. Trust me. Where had she heard that before?

He helped her to the stairs, hand around her waist. She was tired, so tired from the evening's antics, but his support, his touch helped. "Are you sure about this?"

"Don't worry. And Emma, do try to keep an open mind. The world is filled with such amazing possibilities."

It was painful, but she took the first steps back up the staircase that she had ascended so many times that evening.

She didn't look back to see if the young Jack was still behind her. She did, however, feel the strange rush of dizziness that had become a touchstone of this traveling. And when she reached the landing on the second floor outside of the entrance to the house, she heard a familiar voice and felt his hands going around her waist, pulling her up the final steps.

"Emma, are you all right? Your father has been looking for you." She looked up into Jack's face, an older Jack, bearded and mustached. And undeniably the one that she had started the evening with.

Chapter 18

The Wedding

The wedding day moved forward seamlessly, and there were many moments during which Emma continued to ponder the possibility that nothing that was happening was real. At some point, she very well could awake back in her bedroom at Belle Coeur, where she would dress because her aunt seldom afforded her the services of one of her lady's maids, and then descend the grand staircase and immediately attend her aunt in the morning room. It was always early, even before breakfast, when they would discuss how the day would proceed. Yes, she supposed, in some respects, she had moved into the role of a glorified servant, but there was in this the comfort of the predictable.

Here, within the realms of the second possibility, the dream, as she preferred to call it, was calm, soothing in the detached numbness of the emotion. But predictable? Not in the furthest reaches of her existence could she describe what was occurring as predictable. If she were not encased in this strange, mesmerizing blanket of complacency, her heart would be clutched in a wild, fearful panic because, in truth, she was plunging into the abyss of the unknown, the unknowable. So perhaps it was the former, an extended dream. Perhaps all things were a dream, and she, as Emma Lescale, had never truly existed but instead was an imagination within someone else's thought. Even she had to admit how spiraling and insubstantial her own reflections had become.

But today, dream or not, her father had kissed her cheek at the chapel and squeezed her hand as though he cared. It must be artifice, for he really didn't care for her. He had left her alone so young to fend for herself in the hands of so many people who considered her an afterthought, what could loosely be called a consideration that always came after so many others — so many things that took precedence before she did.

She heard the priest's words because she had been raised Catholic, but again, the ritual and the sentiment failed to touch her. She answered as was expected because it did not occur to her not to. Because, after all, there was the strong possibility that this, all of this, was a dream from which she would awaken into some new unforeseen reality, a reality where she wasn't herself at all.

Jack kissed her briefly on her lips after the ceremony and then took her hand in his, his arm about her waist, touching the satin edging decorating the bodice of her traveling suit. She felt her knees giving way, but his strength propped her up, supporting her. He whispered in her ear, "It's all right, Emma," the man, the one who now called himself her husband.

And then they were in a carriage, his carriage heading back to her father's house. She looked out the window, trying to draw in air she felt utterly bereft of. He patted her knee, and she turned back to him. "I know this feels overwhelming, Emma." She looked at him strangely. The problem was that she wasn't feeling at all, but rather floating, somewhat disconnected from what she should be feeling.

"Yes, I suppose," she answered because she should indeed say something.

He looked, well, not terribly surprised though attentive, you might say. "We'll take things slow," he said a bit methodically.

Things, she wondered, with distraction. Oh yes, he must be referring to the business of marriage, the intimacy shared between a husband and wife. She nodded slightly and turned back to the window. She couldn't think, wouldn't consider any of this just now.

✝

He knew without question that it wouldn't be much longer. The energy that Jack had extended to maintain the veil of complacency around Emma was tremendous. She had a formidable will, something which he should have known. He waited downstairs in Nathaniel's study while Mattie helped Emma with some last-minute packing. Some of the things she would take with her for their trip this week to the Gulf Coast, while others would be sent straight to Bienville Street.

Mattie and Benjamin would spend this week resettling Nathaniel and Emma's things into his house. He had left them funds to hire help so that the bulk of the transference would occur while they were gone. Nathaniel's Esplanade Avenue home would have to be sold to settle many of the old man's debts. He took a certain satisfaction in knowing that his friend and mentor's life would be much easier through this marriage.

He sank into a wingback chair. His head throbbed from the expenditure of energy. He was concerned, in fact, more than concerned about what would happen once Emma fully emerged from his influence. In retrospect, it was clear that it would have been better if he had taken more time with the situation. But Nathaniel's escalated deterioration had made that impossible. He owed it to the old man to see that he didn't end up in an asylum somewhere.

He breathed deeply, trying to clear his mind, visualizing his bride upstairs. He wasn't a beast. He would not try to force anything before she was ready, if indeed she would ever be ready.

He closed his eyes and focused intently. In his mind, he could see her as a young girl asleep in her bed at Belle Coeur. He remembered during one of his meditations, he'd found her there in tears. She felt so ostracized by her relatives and abandoned by the father she'd never known.

He'd used his energy to guide her to calmness. Sleep quickly overcame her. And although it was midday, she had lain in bed surrounded by the comforting energy he'd sent. He used this image as the touchstone to maintain the shroud of calmness around her now.

The truth was that if she were definitively set against him, none of this would work. There was confusion inside her, battling between how she thought things should be and her feelings within. The connection between them, whether acknowledged by her or not, was powerful. This, he was able to use to his advantage. Whether that was a purely honorable move on his part could be debated. But then again, he never considered himself a wholly honorable or pure man. He made choices that he deemed expedient, like lulling his new bride into acceptance of their wedding.

There was that weighty question; however, that remained. What was going to happen when she realized it?

⚜

They took the train from New Orleans to the Mississippi Gulf Coast. Emma had never traveled by train before. In fact, coming to New Orleans was the first time she had traveled by riverboat. It was an odd, uneasy feeling leaving her father's house. Mattie seemed more emotional than she, hugging her tightly upstairs, asking her shakily if she thought they'd all be happy living at Dr. Jack's house on Bienville Street.

She smiled and reassured her, unsure if what she said was true. Would they? Would she be happy? What did that feel like to be happy? And then she remembered planting flowers with Jack in her father's garden, and she recalled the laughter, the warmth of the sun.

Yes, that was what happiness felt like.

They were journeying to the Magnolia Inn, a lovely little establishment in Biloxi just a short walk away from the beachfront, or so she'd been told. Jack had held her hand warmly, explaining that this time would be a chance for her to rest, for them to make plans.

Rest from what exactly she thought to ask but did not. What sort of plans, she pondered. Part of her was still convinced that this was unreal, a dream, and at any given moment, she would awaken. Because in real life, in her own life, she would have never married Jack Fallon. She would never have married anyone, although she did trust Jack more than most, and he did have this peculiar way of setting things right, even when things felt so turned around.

She enjoyed the train ride, though she was overcome with the most overwhelming wave of sleepiness. Sitting next to her, Jack insisted that she put her head on his shoulder. She supposed that when she awoke, all of this would be different. And it was unfortunate. It was a pleasant dream. She hadn't minded much of what had occurred, only that it simply wasn't possible. She wasn't Emma Fallon. She just couldn't be.

❧

He hoped that it would be a pleasant week for the two of them, hoped rather than believed. Of course, he could feel it at once when his control snapped, or should he say waned?

She was quiet, saying very little when she awoke, just a bit wide-eyed as though absorbing all around her. They disembarked the train and obtained a hackney. He asked her if she was well, and she nodded with distraction, continuing to look around with her lovely green eyes. But there was no verbal response, and he could feel it acutely on his skin, in his mind. She was puzzling things out.

He did notice as they waited for their luggage to be unloaded, she was preoccupied. Emma glanced down at her ring finger, noting with serious attention the delicate gold band next to the blue sapphire — the one that he had placed on her hand earlier in the day.

And then, he saw her eyes focusing on something off in the distance as though contemplating visions unseen by those around her.

He had a lot of work to do. He realized this as he studied his wife standing quietly beside him. She was beautiful. That was undeniable, complex — an aspect that attracted and intrigued him. Jack Fallon never avoided a challenge. That was not his way, particularly one that meant so much to him.

⚜

It was a lovely hotel, a large, sprawling white wood-framed structure. From the enormous echoing central hallway, they were brought to a two-room suite on the second floor with a French door between the front sitting room and the bedroom, as well as a private door leading out to a lovely gallery facing the coast. Within the bedroom was a beautiful dark wood canopy bed, perhaps mahogany or oak, she thought distractedly. And the picture window overlooked the sandy beach dunes in the distance. It was lovely, enchanting, quite unlike any place she'd been to before. After they registered, an employee had quickly settled their luggage at the foot of the bed on a bench.

And as it was, despite her surroundings, Emma sat quietly on the quilted bedspread, feeling the first pains of a headache beginning to creep up her neck and start shooting sparks of pain to her temples. She assumed the anxiety of the quick rush of events had brought it on. But strangely, she didn't remember feeling anxious at all, not feeling much of anything until now. It was true that she did have a history of such calamitous headaches. The first she remembered was when she was a young child, overhearing the La Maire girls making fun of her.

"*Poor little orphan,*" they chanted. "*Nobody wants her.*" And then, soon after, the headache ensued. Of course, it was connected to emotions, intense emotions.

She glanced around the room. It was spacious, with several chairs, a dresser, and the door to the lavatory. There were soft touches — a vase on a table with pink roses and baby's breath, pink against that dark furniture, nearly black. Behind her eyes, she could feel the pressure mounting. She stared pensively out the window with the lovely seaside view. It was still light but perhaps just beginning to dim a bit. She had no idea what time it was. Jack had gone out to stretch his legs. She told him that she wanted to rest. But she hadn't, not really, just sat on the edge of the canopy bed, realizing, understanding finally that indeed all of this was no dream. This was all too real.

She rubbed her temples. What did she usually do to rid herself of the headache?

Josie, her Aunt Adeleine's maid, had told her to put a hot towel over her eyes in sleep, long uninterrupted sleep in a darkened room. Of course, Jack was a doctor. Perhaps he would know what to do. If she told him, but should she? He was her husband now. She'd actually married him. Somehow, she'd stumbled into this, all of this, not really meaning to.

She heard the door to the sitting room open. The sound sent a dart of pain right through her eye. She covered them, rubbing them both.

"She must be exaggerating. She's not really sick." She heard her aunt say.

"No, ma'am, it's real. My mother suffered in the same way. There's nothing to be done. Just wait it out." Josie had been kind, and kindness should always be cherished.

"Emma, what's wrong?"

She removed her hands that had been covering her eyes. Her vision had become a bit blurry, something that came inevitably with what Josie called the megrim headaches.

She shook her head, rubbing her temples as she felt him beside her with his arm around her. "A headache," she murmured. "I get them sometimes, very bad," she managed to say with difficulty. She could feel him, checking the temperature of her forehead, taking her wrist, and feeling her pulse.

"I brought my medical bag. I have something in there that will help you rest."

She nodded. She knew there were things she needed to tell him about the marriage, about the confusion, the mistake she'd made. But the pain was too bad, descending too quickly. Perhaps if she slept, it wouldn't be so difficult when she woke up.

Chapter 19

The Bridal Trip

I t was not good. It had snapped, the influence, and he pre-ferred to say influence because the word control hit him somewhat distastefully. He hadn't anticipated how much internal pressure would be exerted on Emma by what he was doing, that it would become a physical manifestation. He should have anticipated the potential for such a side effect. But he had been so absorbed with obtaining the goal that he hadn't consid-ered such consequences.

It had been a colossal error of judgment on his part. But Jack had seen no alternative at the time. Nathaniel's condition was deteriorating rapidly, as were the old man's finances. Within a month, debt collectors would have thrown Emma and her father out of their house. As it was, most of its sale would most certainly go to settling what Nathaniel's owed. He needed to protect them, to protect them both. A marriage would ensure this, and he hadn't had the luxury of time to woo Emma Lescale properly and convince her of this fact. So instead, once he evaluated the situation's complexities, he took these measures, measures that if she recognized, she could and probably would hate him for.

But he'd acted, nonetheless. Some might say the decision had come to him rather quickly, impulsively, but in his mind, the facts simply coalesced rapidly. And he decided what must be done. He'd used a great deal of focused energy to bring Emma with him to travel to the *Between*. It was a technique from his esoteric studies that he'd practiced consistently over the three years, and actually even before, he'd lived in the Bienville Street house. What he hadn't realized was that once he'd initiated the transition, Emma would so quickly have the ability to travel on her own, uncontrolled as it might be. It had happened once when they'd first begun. He'd lost track of her, then again when she encountered George Battiste, and once more after the parasites. He supposed he shouldn't be surprised, considering whose daughter she was, but the blind reactiveness of it worried him. She was clearly gifted in this, but so had Nathaniel been. He'd been determined and reckless, Jack firmly believed, resulting in his present state of infirmity.

He had concentrated intently, focusing on Emma's where-abouts. Undoubtedly, the parasites had frightened her, driven her to an emotional outburst, and then the uncharted traveling. Clearly, exposing her to all of this with no preparation had been a colossal error. He had needed to get things under control again.

And that was when this decision was made.

But in truth, this course of action hadn't been wholly solidi-fied in his mind until the day after the dinner party when he'd met Emma in the courtyard. He had decided then that it was essential to push the engagement forward. After all, she had agreed or seemed not so set against it under less than traditional circumstances. But her state of confusion and the indecision on her part worried him. If he could get her to marry him, the power of the marriage ceremony, the energy created, and the protective bonds put in place would stabilize things and help her, possibly both of them, in ways she wouldn't understand. But he did. He understood what they could be together. He'd already seen it.

So that day, in Nathaniel's courtyard, he'd begun to exert his influence and continued to do so until now.

She lay in the darkened bedroom, tossing and turning in the tortured sleep that she'd been caught up in. He had managed to remove her dress with some difficulty, taking off the corset and leaving her in the light camisole shift she'd been wearing beneath. He'd given her a light dose of laudanum for the pain and, hopefully, to help her rest more easily. But clearly, it wasn't a comfortable sleep. Several times during the night, she'd called out frantically for her mother, a mother she'd never known.

It was well past two in the morning already. Jack had given up on rest sometime before. He sipped a now quite warm glass of champagne. The bottle had been delivered as a courtesy of the Magnolia Hotel earlier that evening. He'd mentioned when they arrived that they were on their bridal trip. That, however, now felt like a thousand years ago. Strange, he'd felt hope then, hope that things might turn out quite differently. Maybe Emma might suddenly discover that she liked the idea of being married to him. And maybe she might one day come to love him as he loved her, as he had loved her long before they met when he felt the wistful loneliness of that little girl thrust into life amongst unfeeling relatives. She didn't fit there, especially not in that shadowed house. Too many had no conception of how dark a shroud past events could place around and within a structure. And Emma was too different, unique, not to feel this within Belle Coeur, too sharp, intuitive, and sensitive. So, she had built her walls around her just to survive.

Jack understood this, for he was much the same way with so little in common with the people he'd encountered, colleagues, patients, acquaintances in college and later work. He often felt he was an aberrant species but pretended to be like them — except, of course, with Nathaniel, and then when he discovered Emma. They were kindred. And now he'd hurt her, truly not meaning to.

He put down the glass of champagne and removed his jacket and vest, laying them across a nearby chair in the sitting room. He rolled up his shirt sleeves and opened the black leather doctor's bag on the cherry wood end table. Within, he fished out a small vial of liquid that lay tucked away in one of the interior side pockets.

It was something he'd concocted himself — a combination of oils, perhaps less than orthodox, but including lavender as well as other natural substances for purposes of sedation.

Quietly, he walked into the darkened space. Light from the sitting room illuminated the shadows to a minuscule degree.

Emma continued to move around restlessly. He opened the vial, putting some on both sets of his first two fingertips, then placing the unused portion on the bedside table.

Without a word, he leaned over the bed, touching her temples, rubbing gently. She murmured, but he continued to massage as the oil entered her skin, softly repeating words of an ancient language that was no longer used by anyone. He could feel her calming a bit, relaxing beneath his ministrations. When he was satisfied that he'd helped, he stopped, then bending down to remove his shoes. He took a deep breath and climbed into bed with his new wife, pulling her against his chest in a comforting embrace. He felt her still for a moment, then relax against him. Whether she would acknowledge this or not, they were in this together now. And he would see them through, wherever it might lead.

⚜

It was always difficult for her to emerge through one of these episodes, as Aunt Adeleine had termed it. It wasn't as if all of a sudden, the discomfort was gone, and everything was well. The pain in her head, behind her eyes, would usually mutate from a pervasive throbbing into a dull ache. This ache, of course, would be accompanied by blurry vision for several hours, and that worn-out feeling akin to someone who had recently been washed up on a beach after a shipwreck.

This morning felt much in accordance with her usual experience, with one exception. She woke up in the very warm and comforting embrace of her new husband.

She shifted a bit, so disoriented that she couldn't fathom at first where she was. And then it filtered back in — the dream. In the dream, she'd gone to a chapel connected to a larger church on St. Charles Avenue. She was in a traveling suit, dark brown wool accented by satin and lace, pragmatic but flattering. And there, she had pledged to be the wife of Dr. James Fallon.

She moved cautiously in the large canopy bed. She was lying against his chest, his shirt unbuttoned to nearly the waist. She could hear his light breathing. He still slept.

It wasn't a dream. This understanding filtered strongly through the dull ache in her head. She tried to gently extricate herself from the embrace. It wasn't as though it was uncomfortable. Clearly, she had slept some hours in great relaxation, being held by him. It was just that her mind continued to reject this reality. She sat up, glancing around the room. She didn't recognize it. But draped across a nearby chair was the afternoon dress, the one tailored with the deep blue bodice she'd changed into after they'd arrived here, and some other undergarments that belonged to her. It was the dream that she was now acknowledging in the harsh light of day was no dream.

Her head spun with dizziness. Then she looked down, recognizing that she was only wearing her shift. Had they been intimate? She didn't remember that. Was that why he was holding her so close when she awoke? She couldn't recall, only blinding pain in her head.

She took a sharp breath, rubbing her eyes, trying to clear some of the blurriness in her vision that she was still experiencing. And then she felt movement beside her and a hand on her arm. "Emma," he said softly. "How are you feeling?"

She felt a rampant blush steal over her face. He was in bed with her. She couldn't remember having anyone in bed with her before, ever. But it seemed that she had indeed married him.

"I don't know," she murmured, not meeting his gaze. How could she answer, not knowing much of anything?

"You were ill last night," he said, squeezing her arm a bit. Perhaps in reassurance, she thought.

"I was?" she asked. She remembered the pain, the grueling, unrelenting pain in her head.

Softly, his hand moved up to her chin, gently turning her gaze to face him. She drew a breath. He was a bit disheveled, his hair not so neatly combed, his eyes a bit glazed, and the unbuttoned shirt revealing his muscular chest, covered by a scattering of dark blonde hair. He was a handsome man in so many ways and, more than that, a compelling one. There was that quality in him that drew her so strongly. That, in this moment, with his proximity, frightened her immensely.

"You were very ill last night. It seemed to be some sort of a migraine."

She nodded slightly as he dropped his hand from her chin. He had what he wanted, her attention. "Yes, I used to get terrible headaches occasionally at my aunt's house."

"Well, a lot has happened quickly. It's possible the exertion of events brought it on. I gave you some laudanum last night to help you sleep."

"You did?" she said.

"You don't remember?"

She shook her head, and she shouldn't have. It was still very sensitive. "No, so many things feel like a blur, unreal, I would say. I don't even remember getting undressed," she said, turning away again.

"I undressed you," he said rather flatly as though it was a completely natural thing for him to do. "I thought you would be more comfortable."

She nodded again, strangely imagining what that must have felt like, his hands on her, undressing her. Still battling with that encroaching blush, she wondered with distraction what else would change now that she was Mrs. Fallon. "I –" she began, not knowing exactly how to voice this, "Jack, there must be something wrong with me." Again, he squeezed her arm, but she was looking down, wouldn't look at him, couldn't just now. "I feel as though my mind has been in a sort of fog. The wedding, before it, and things that I remember from your house, they didn't feel real — like a sort of strange dream. But then, when I woke up this morning, and you were here next to me, I realized it was all true."

And then, almost in a fluid motion, he pulled her into his arms again, her back against his chest so that she could feel his warm skin through the very thin material of her shift. "We just need to give things time, Emma. I promise I'll be a good husband to you. And I won't pressure you into anything you aren't ready for." He softly kissed the top of her head. It seemed that he wasn't really listening to her, and she wondered if this was also to be the way of things now.

Chapter 20

The Marriage

He was mindful to tread carefully. For the first few days of their week away, he concentrated on making sure that Emma recovered her health. He had breakfast brought to their room — tea and biscuits — and ensured that she rested most of the day. Ostensibly, he was a perfect gentleman, patiently caring for his new wife. He hoped fervently that she would simply let go of her confusion about how they got to this place and accept that they were married now, accept that he was her loving husband. He hoped rather than believed that this would be the course of things. She was quiet, and he attributed this to ill health, but something within also told him that she was weighing things, considering. And knowing from his instincts and exposure to her how fiercely intelligent she was, well, this made him nervous.

So, Jack found himself in the precarious position of warring with himself — caught between the proper inclination to simply give Emma time to adjust to her new status as his wife and another inclination — the one urging him on a different path. Truthfully, in many regards, it would solve most of his problems. He felt quite inclined to seduce his wife.

Besides the fact that it would quell the mounting desire that he battled living in such proximity with the woman he not only was in love with but also wanted carnally very badly, it would solidify the union if it were consummated. It was a growing impulse, not unlike his sudden decision to yank her into a nearby dimension during the dinner party at his house. Of course, he dutifully reminded himself of how that inclination did not turn out quite as well as he had planned.

So instead, he worked quite strenuously, to quell his impulsiveness and be patient with her. But it was difficult. He wasn't a man who indulged in lying to himself. This marriage was not wholly altruistic. He didn't marry Emma to simply protect Nathaniel. He married Emma because he wanted Emma. But he couldn't just play the quick game. He had to play the smart game.

The third day seemed better. She allowed him to help her dress so that they could go for a walk along the beach. She still seemed pale and a bit shaky but was much improved than she had been during and after the migraine episode.

Last night, he slept next to her in the bed. She had watched him get in a bit wide-eyed but said nothing. And today, she allowed him to help her with the buttons on her gray walking dress and to brush out her long blonde hair before she twisted it up into the low chignon bun that was her usual style.

His fingers brushed the nape of her neck, and he could feel a response, though she said nothing.

On their walk, she took his arm occasionally, and they spoke little.

"Are you all right, Emma?" he asked.

"It's lovely here. I've never been to a place like this," she said a little distantly.

"You know, I dearly want you to be happy." She nodded and smiled a bit but didn't respond.

That evening, they had dinner in the main dining room, although she ate little and pleaded fatigue for an early evening.

Jack stayed up later in the sitting room, reading a book he'd brought. He was restless and feared that he'd only keep her awake if he retired with her.

He questioned things deeply, wondering if they could ever get past this peculiar place of impasse that they seemed to be stuck in.

⚜

She wanted to go home. The only problem was that she had no idea what home looked like anymore. Being near the water at the Magnolia Hotel was soothing in some respects, particularly when they walked along the beach. She could feel herself relax and not worry, allowing all the anxieties that seemed to want to plague her simply drop away. She had never before truly understood the solace that came with the mind that was no longer consumed with thought. There was peace in simply not knowing, even if one was poised on the edge of a precipice. If you did not know that the next step would be the one that plunged you into desolation, then there could be quiet, tremulous as it was.

"I'd like to go back."

He glanced up from the book that he had been reading. They were taking afternoon tea in their room after a long walk on the beach. He looked at her with contemplation for a moment, then responded. "I thought you liked it here."

She swallowed on a dry, nervous throat. They had been here just over four days, spending calm, uncomplicated time together, visiting shops in the small coastal cities of Biloxi and Ocean Springs, and in the evenings dining in the restaurant at the heart of the hotel, then retiring — she first, then Jack sometime later when she was asleep. It was an odd pattern of avoidance that they had sunk into, not speaking of things that were of much significance, not seeming to want to.

"It's lovely, Jack, very soothing. But we both know that this isn't a bridal trip in any conventional sense."

He slowly closed his book, laying it down on a nearby table. "Would you like it to be?"

She breathed in a bit, sharply scrambling at his directness but also trying to remember exactly what she wanted to say. "What I would like is to go back now. I will be blunt with you, Jack. I never intended to marry, to marry anyone. And yet here we are, and, in all honesty, I can't account for it. I can't explain why, for a time, it seemed that I changed my mind and allowed events to move forward, although it seems that I did. So, all I can see now is to get on with it."

"Get on with it?" He repeated rather slowly and deliberately, though clearly questioning what she meant.

"I mean, go back and see what sort of life there will be now. That is, if you are sure that you want to go forward with this marriage. I mean, we haven't — so legally, we could probably."

"Consummated the union," he said with little emotion.

"Yes," she answered, a bit flustered at his bold description of what had not occurred between them.

"No," he said with little expression.

"No," she whispered. "No, you mean that—"

"No, I do not want an annulment. I want to go forward with the marriage."

His flat pronouncement felt as though it knocked the wind out of her. "I see," she murmured. "But this can't be what you really want, Jack."

"No, it's not, Emma, but I did promise to be patient and give things time. So, if you're ready to return, I will make the arrangements."

"Yes, thank you." She should have felt relieved at that point because she had taken control, at least a bit. Although to what end she had no idea, oddly, all she felt was further anxiety, anxiety about an unknown future that stretched out before her. And truly, she was not unconvinced that she was indeed somehow poised on the very edge of that unacknowledged precipice.

✣

The house, Jack's house, which was now her new home, was filled with phantoms, elusive phantoms that seemed intent on floating about her mind. For not the first time, Emma — for somewhere along the way, she had entirely shed her childhood and Belle Coeur designation of Emmeline — questioned and considered if it was possible that she'd experienced some sort of mental break, a psychological crumbling of some sort.

Even just crossing the threshold on Bienville Street, she felt as though there were ghosts here, phantoms, memories that she could almost touch but were separated from her by some thin intangible veil. She stood in the courtyard as Benjamin unloaded the luggage. He had arrived with the carriage not so very long ago at the train station, helping them disembark.

But just being back here, standing so still in the courtyard, was bringing back a flood of images that felt familiar and foreign at the same time. It had been that night, the night of the dinner, that now felt like a lifetime ago. She and Jack were sitting in this very courtyard, and he was explaining quite clearly why he needed her to marry him.

She felt his arm go around her shoulders, and the contact jolted her out of the curiously fragmented recollection. "Are you all right, Emma?" he asked. But she could see his face back then, so serious, so determined that night, as if what he was suggesting was more than reasonable.

"Yes, just tired," she murmured.

"Then I'll take you to your room," he said softly.

"Where is Nathaniel?" she asked as they ascended the staircase to the house's second floor. Also, this staircase, she remembered it from that night. There was the strange dizziness, then another man — someone she'd run into.

"He's resting. I've hired a nurse from the Hotel Dieu to attend to his needs. I set up rooms for him in the garçonnière, very similar to his study back home. You can see him later if you like."

She could see him later with his permission, she thought with distraction. She questioned whether Jack would be controlling her access to her father now, now that he had mastery over everything.

He led her down the hallway toward the front of the house. She knew his rooms were here, and she wondered with nervousness if that was where he was bringing her. But instead, he opened another door, and she was relieved to find much of her furniture from her father's house. It occurred to her that Jack must've given very specific orders while they were gone to have this arranged so quickly.

"I thought you'd be more comfortable here for now, Emma," he said as she walked within. It flashed across her mind, the same room but a canopied bed, a mahogany wardrobe, and Jack. Jack had been kissing her with unrestrained passion.

She focused on what was before her, lightly running her fingers along the surface of the cherry wood dresser as though she were greeting an old friend. "Yes, Jack, I do appreciate this," she said, genuinely pleased or rather genuinely relieved.

He stood in the doorway, quietly watching her. Then she noticed another small door on the side of the far wall. "Where does that lead?" She said impulsively, not considering the possible ramifications of the inquiry.

"To my bedroom. These rooms are connected."

"Oh," she murmured.

"Emma, I simply sought to give you time to adjust to your new circumstances. I am not interested in a marriage in name only."

His directness felt a bit like an impact somewhere in the vicinity of her stomach. Not wholly unpleasant, just powerfully disturbing. Her new husband was very determined, patient as he might be. She needed to remember that. "I understand, Jack," she said lightly. "And I appreciate all you are doing."

He looked at her pensively as though he was considering her comment. "Well then, I'll let you rest. It's my dearest wish that you are happy here, Emma, in your new home."

She smiled slightly, determined to keep things as affable as possible. "Thank you, Jack, that is my wish as well."

Chapter 21

The Garçonnière

The old French name for the outbuilding situated some-what perpendicular to the main structure in the Creole townhouse was the garçonnière. It was so named as a separate residence for young men who wanted some independence from their families. And once Jack purchased the residence, he found that he liked the designation. So, he used it.

He ventured in that direction after his uncomfortable exchange with Emma. He hadn't spent much time considering their situation or how exactly they would move forward after the wedding. All his energies had been spent on simply accomplishing the marriage, which, up until the moment the final vows were exchanged, he had no real certainty or conviction that would happen at all. But it did. It was accomplished, and now they were stumbling around in uncharted territory. He gave himself solace in the belief that somewhere deep within her, Emma was not entirely opposed to the match, or he would not have been able to sway her to it. That is what he told himself, but of course, there were always doubts, doubts that at times felt as though they would wholly consume his peace of mind.

He ascended the steps of the garçonniere to the second floor. It was a rather large building. The ground floor housed Mattie and Benjamin, as well as the house's kitchen. Upstairs, he had arranged a suite of rooms for Nathaniel and a separate room for the nurse he had employed to take care of him and monitor his condition.

He dearly hoped his old friend would adjust well to the accommodations. He should be comfortable and well cared for, but at enough distance to allow privacy for the occupants of the main house. Without question, that was something that he felt they were in dire need of just now.

He lightly tapped on the outside door, waiting only moments before he walked inside. The first room was a large one he'd converted into Nathaniel's study. It was filled with bookshelves packed with volumes he had moved from the Esplanade house, as well as many of the pieces of furniture that could comfortably fit. His friend was seated behind his desk, reading glasses on, and engrossed in some book. There was a small fire in the fireplace against the wall. He would have to mention this to Amelia Clay, Nathaniel's nurse, to keep her eye on it. With Nathaniel's mood swings as of late, he wanted to keep any potentially dangerous scenarios well in check.

"I knocked, Nathaniel. I hope that I'm not intruding."

He looked up from his reading, his eyes seeming a little glazed as he took off his glasses and placed them absently on the desk. This desk, Jack, was indeed most pleased about. It did fit perfectly in the room, and he felt keenly that Nathaniel would take great comfort in its presence. "Sorry, Jack, I didn't hear you. I was rereading this book on medieval alchemy. Do you remember it?"

He sat down in a nearby chair, smiling. Perhaps this might be one of his more lucid days. "Yes, I do. Excellent work."

"I think so too. I was trying to retrace where we might have gone wrong in our work, perhaps the transmutation of energy. There should have been a way to harness it more completely."

Jack breathed in deeply. This wasn't an area he wanted to reopen with Nathaniel in his current state of mind. Delving into such experiments so rashly, he suspected, had brought on an accelerated deterioration of his friend's mental state. As he recalled, everything happened so quickly, and Nathaniel had always been determined to plunge forward unfettered.

"Perhaps we should proceed more carefully, Nathaniel."

"No, no, we are sufficiently prepared. We cannot always be so cautious, Jack. That is not the way to greatness."

He'd been wrong, of course. New frontiers should be explored with trepidation, not rushed into unthinkingly. But he was a younger man when they'd begun, and he knew that their colleagues in The Society of Magnetism would indeed plunge forward if they realized what direction he and Nathaniel had taken their research. Extrapolating from mesmerism used in surgery and clinical procedures to full-out dimensional travelling using natural energy bands was quite a jump. And as it was, maybe it had been too far a jump that they'd taken, given Nathaniel's current condition. But then again, his mentor had pushed hard against any constraints, reaching into realms that Jack believed now should have been left well enough alone.

He brought himself to the present, focusing on the man before him. "Nathaniel, I wanted to find out if you feel comfortable in these rooms."

The old man stared at him for a moment as though trying to process what Jack had said. "This is your house, isn't it, Jack?" He responded slowly.

It was painful, seeing him so disoriented. "Yes, Nathaniel, Emma, and I have married. And you have moved in with us."

He straightened up a bit in the leather chair behind the mahogany desk, almost with surprise. It was the short-term memory that seemed most affected. Although his new situation had been explained to him many times, its retention seemed to elude Nathaniel. "Was that entirely necessary?" he asked, honestly seeming confused.

And at that moment, Jack wasn't at all sure if Nathaniel was referring to the move to Jack's residence or his marriage to his daughter, Emma, or both, perhaps. "Yes, Nathaniel, it was the best thing for all of us," he stated calmly, hopefully to potentially brush aside concerns for both events. And then his old friend slowly nodded, his gaze returning to the book in front of him. "Emma was hoping to see you today if that's all right," he added.

And then his stare returned to Jack, focusing on him a bit more intently, he thought. "And is Emma happy, being married now?"

Jack frowned a bit. That question did seem to get to the heart of the matter. And speaking of rushing in unthinkingly, he'd wondered, not the first time, if he had pushed her too hard, too soon. And what consequence might that ultimately yield in the end?

But his old friend was perceptive and expectantly waiting for an answer, even in his deteriorating mental state. So, he tried to respond honestly, "It's all new to both of us. I very much want to make her happy, but it seems more complicated than I thought it would be."

And then Nathaniel's eyes seemed to soften a bit in that compassionate way that Jack remembered from long ago. "Well, give it time, my boy. Any woman would be more than fortunate to have you. And my Emma is no fool."

⚜

Emma was remembering things, strange things that made no sense. She could envision Jack, but not as he is now. He was older and then, at other times, much younger, talking to her as if both versions knew her so well. And then there were other things, running and then stumbling. There was that person she remembered with a garish face and something else as well — a strange creature — insect-looking. All of these images couldn't possibly be real and made her feel as though she was somehow unraveling, a product of a mental disturbance or even full-blown madness. And more than even the memories, this possibility disturbed her greatly. Had she inherited some malady from Nathaniel? Would Jack be forced to care for her as well as her father as she slipped into some sort of demented state?

But that wasn't all. There were other things, other wisps of peculiar memory. In them, Jack was talking to her, so calmly, about traveling into another place, close to this one but not the same.

She sat up in her bed, her head pounding. She needed to stay calm, or she would bring on another headache. She couldn't handle that right now on top of everything else.

But she also couldn't seem to stop them. The questions continued to flow forward unchecked. Were these indeed some sort of delusions her mind had concocted? They had a strange, foggy quality to them, not at all like an ordinary memory.

Emma reached impulsively for a shawl that she had tossed onto the foot of the bed and wrapped herself in it. She wasn't mad. She wouldn't believe herself to be so. But then again, it crossed her mind that people who were insane probably didn't believe themselves to be so, either.

She lay back in the bed, closing her eyes. Well, this was the best she could do for now. Until convinced otherwise, she would consider herself quite rational and look for other, more reasonable explanations.

Chapter 22

Being Lulled

In a way, she wanted to be unhappy in this new situation, but the truth was that Emma wasn't. Life had settled down into a strange sort of rhythm on Bienville Street. After the week of their bridal trip was over, Jack returned to working at the hospitals in the city. His hours varied, sometimes rather short and sometimes later into the evening. Although he didn't take private patients at the house or in any office, he did make house calls to special clients — some well-off, some not. And more than anything, she was finding that there was much that she didn't know about her new husband.

One thing she did discover was that Jack, like her, wrote volumes and volumes of private journals that he kept under lock and key. She had learned that connected to the main bedroom was a sort of sitting room, not terribly large, that he'd converted into a private study. Sometimes she would hear him in there, for her room was right next to his bedroom, and at other times, she sensed rather than knew that he was in the front parlor. She could feel him there, oddly pacing, and at other times quiet, perhaps reading, perhaps not. But what her new husband didn't do in their first few weeks of marriage was approach her door.

In the evening, Jack would bid her good night at the entrance to her bedroom, often softly kissing her on the cheek, but nothing more. Undeniably, he was handling her cautiously, and that in itself made her uneasy. If she simply relaxed into this pleasant little life here, what would happen to her? Would she be caught completely unaware by something unexpected? She couldn't afford to be lulled, to become comfortable and accepting of this new life. If her time at Belle Coeur had taught her anything, it was not to be complacent lest the unthinkable rear its ugly head and security be stripped away. She had not been complacent since she was quite the little girl when she'd first heard her aunt and the La Maire sisters whispering behind her back.

She could not trust this new life or Jack Fallon, although, in addition to all of this, he had begun to slowly relinquish the running of the house to Emma. Here, there were four servants, well, three servants and a nurse living with them: Mattie and Benjamin, and a middle-aged woman named Hilda who served as a cook and general housekeeper. From what she gathered, she was a lady Jack had met during one of his visits to Charity Hospital. Sadly, she had lost her entire family in a fire and had no place to live. She had been working in the kitchen at the hospital in exchange for having a place to stay in one of the wards at night. Jack had known her for years, but once he married Emma, he decided to see if she wanted to stay with them as a cook and housekeeper.

Hilda was a taciturn woman with skin of a rich umber color, and almost immediately she took to conferring with Emma about meals and strategies for the house. She took Mattie under her wing, and they worked as a team, always giving the appropriate deference to Emma. And, of course, there was the nurse as well, her father's nurse, Amelia Clay. Amelia was a childless widow who, though pleasantly tempered, reported directly and only to Jack, overseeing her father's care. That was the one aspect of living on Bienville Street that did irritate her. It seemed that she could scarcely get a scrap of information out of the dignified, tawny-skinned woman, who was about twenty-five to thirty years Emma's senior. When asked directly about his care, his medication, or much of anything, the answer continued to be — "I'm afraid you'll have to ask your husband this. I've been given strict orders that everything concerning Mr. Nathaniel is confidential."

This was an annoyance that began to gnaw at her. All else seemed so nice, pleasant, and easy, except for this irritation. "I don't know if I like her." She spat out late one evening after dinner. Jack was in the parlor having a brandy, and instead of retiring, as was her custom, she approached him a bit abruptly.

He looked up with some surprise from the papers he had been reading at the small mahogany desk in the corner of the room. "I assure you that Amelia is very competent. Her experience is extensive, and we were lucky to hire her as a private nurse."

"But she won't tell me anything," she snapped, pacing the shiny wooden floor of the room. Hilda had definitely improved the luster of these floors and everything else in her new home. But in the evening, in fact, every evening, all the servants seemed to scatter to the winds, never, it seemed, venturing toward the front of the house. It was at night, truly, as though she and Jack lived in this dwelling all alone.

He stared back at her calmly despite her agitated state. "I'm afraid that's my doing. I've demanded total confidentiality from Amelia as a protection for Nathaniel. I don't want any news of his condition leaking out to the public. In his day, he was an extremely well-respected physician."

She took a sharp breath inward. Again, it felt as though he were handling her, and though, on the surface, things appeared easy, it did bother her to unfathomable degrees. "But I am his daughter. His only blood relative, Jack."

He frowned, and oddly, it pleased her. She had ruffled his placid, congenial demeanor. "And you can come to me with any questions or concerns, Emma. After all, I am your husband." He said a shade too sternly.

She stood in the middle of the parlor staring at him with exasperation, and then murmured, "You do like to be in control of things. I am not a child, Jack. And I would appreciate it if you didn't treat me as such."

His expression hardened slightly as though he were struggling to rein in an odd sort of determination, and then, abruptly, he stood up from behind the desk and walked around to her. "I thought I'd like to take you to the French Opera House this Saturday. They are performing Faust. Would you like that?"

Again, she drew a quick breath, feeling as though her modest triumph was being sidelined. She sat down on the sofa, very unsettled by their unresolved conversation. "I don't know. I've never been to an opera. Of course, I know the story, something about an old man selling his soul to the devil." And then she tacked on glumly. "Is that what my father did?"

Sitting beside her, he silently took her hand in his. "Well, if he did, he certainly didn't confide it to me."

"Really, are you sure?" she muttered with annoyance. "I'm sure I don't know what to make of the two of you at times, or us for that matter."

He nodded, seeming unwilling to delve too deeply into any of her comments. "Well, perhaps a little patience is in order, and everything will settle into a situation of your liking in time. So, the opera, Emma, will you go with me? A new experience and all that," he cajoled, squeezing her hand a bit.

Reluctantly, she nodded silently. She still felt vexed, vexed by his evasiveness, and wholly unsatisfied as though something looming, undefinable, continued to bother her, but she couldn't quite pinpoint it. And Jack, well, Jack was continuing to handle her. She could feel it. And she truly hated that. "Pauline wrote to me. She and her husband will be in the city at the beginning of next month. She's heard of our marriage and would like to see us."

"Do you want to see her?" he asked returning to his reading.

"I suppose," she replied with no conviction. "I really have no idea what I want. Truly, I feel a bit lost."

And then he said pointedly, "I do want you to be happy, Emma. I honestly believe you have to give things time. Why don't you take Mattie and go buy a new dress for the opera tomorrow?"

"I have dresses," she answered sullenly.

"Well, buy something new. It's time to change things a bit."

She stood up, responding with little enthusiasm. "All right, Jack, if that's what you truly want."

He frowned ever so slightly, seeming a bit put off by her genuine lack of interest. As she began to leave the room, she heard him call behind her. "Nothing gray, Emma. You have so much gray."

⚜

Once they were there, however, she thought about getting something gray just to spite him. But in perusing the selection at Madame Olympia's boutique on Chartres Street, a lovely rose-colored evening dress of silk and a matching shawl beckoned her. But she did hesitate. It was so feminine, not really like her at all, but Mattie, her companion for the day, pushed her with a single-mindedness that greatly surprised her.

"It's perfect, Miss. That shade brings out a lovely, flushed color in your skin."

She hesitated. She didn't want to feel foolish. The worst thing for her was to feel foolish. Pauline would have done justice to such a dress, but not Emma. She had always felt older, more matronly, even as a young child. She simply did have an old soul, or perhaps a young one that had just been formidably suppressed into thinking it was old.

"I don't know, Mattie. I truly think I'm not young enough to wear this shade."

And with that, her youthful companion let out a short laugh. "Nonsense, Miss Emma, you are still a young woman and so beautiful, though I rather think you take too many pains to hide it."

"Of course, I don't," she muttered nervously in a way that felt convincing to no one, most particularly herself.

"And I do know Dr. Jack would love you in this."

She wondered if that was true, staring at her reflection in the dressing room mirror. In truth, it wasn't overly lacy or really too immature. The lines of the gown were clean, sloping down to a somewhat fitted bodice. With the matching shawl, it would be more than appropriate for their outing.

"I don't know," she murmured out loud, not really to Mattie, not really to anyone in particular except herself. "I just don't know why he wanted to marry me at all," she said to the tall, sedate blonde woman staring back at her from the mirror. What a stranger she was to her, so poised, so constrained, not at all as she felt inside.

"What was that, Miss?" Mattie asked her. Had she said that aloud? She hadn't really realized it.

"I suppose I'll take this one."

And the young servant girl seemed genuinely pleased for some reason, some reason that eluded Emma completely.

Chapter 23

The Opera

I t was odd that after a certain hour in the evening, the servants would disappear from the main house. Mattie would be present to help her dress in the morning but never help her later. Emma thought to mention this to Jack, but she didn't. Instead, she tried to manage, though she knew undoing some of the back buttons on the rose-colored gown she'd worn tonight might take an extra effort.

The evening itself at the opera had been quite remarkable, wonderful, in fact. Jack had summoned a handsome cab and did seem delighted with the gown she had selected at Madame Olympia's. He was charming and attentive, and she couldn't deny that she found it a little unnerving. She wasn't used to that sort of attention from a man. She certainly didn't trust it.

The concerning point, at least in her mind, was that he treated her as someone she did not know herself to be. She was not beautiful, although he acted as though she was. She was not entertaining, although he seemed to be thoroughly captivated by her ideas and thoughts. She was not funny, although he did seem to find amusement with her. She curtly and often reminded herself that this was not a love match but rather a marriage of convenience. Because during the course of the evening, it was so easy to forget these truths that she had always layered reality with.

Tonight, it felt natural to lose herself in another existence, one where she was adored. It was intoxicating and so very dangerous.

They attended the opera, her first opera. The French Opera House on Bourbon Street was an imposing structure, Greek Revival in style, towering over everything in its vicinity like some sort of Colossus. Within the hall, the building was equally impressive, decorated with enormous Corinthian columns and a grand elliptical auditorium arranged with a color scheme of red and white. She and Jack were seated amongst the central tiers of seats, but around them were rows of lattice and open boxes clearly reserved for special patrons.

The presentation was Faust, and throughout the performance, Emma found herself sinking into another place, allowing her imagination to take flight — the music, the singing, the sweeping artistry of her surroundings. Here, it was easy to forget who she was because she felt utterly transformed. So many times through the performance, Jack took her hand and held it, and more than once bringing her hand up to his lips and quickly kissing it. It was as though he could feel her excitement. Then, when the performance was over, he attentively escorted her outside into the cool night air and back to the carriage.

"Did you enjoy it?" He whispered into her ear.

Everything still felt so unreal, as though she had stepped into someone else's life, perhaps out of a book she once read closeted up in her attic room at Belle Coeur. And she was reticent to let go of the excitement that was still coursing through her. It was all too dizzying for her to disguise her adulation. "It was exceptional, Jack, truly wonderful," she replied. And he seemed pleased, genuinely delighted by her reaction. Inside the carriage, he sat next to her, closer than when they had traveled to the opera house. And he put his arm around her and said softly, "It is my intention for you to be happy, Emma, always."

And then he tilted her face to his and kissed her, so gently and then more, more passionately, so that she couldn't help but feel that she was melting against him.

On Bienville Street, Benjamin came out into the courtyard when they arrived, but it was Jack who helped her out of the handsome cab — his hand on her arm, her waist, her back. It was as if he made an effort to continue touching her.

"Why don't you wait for me in the parlor, Emma? I'll be up in a moment," he said quietly so that only she would hear.

She nodded quickly in response. It was not considered, just instinctive. How could she not agree after the evening they'd spent together, after the bubbling rush of emotions swirling through her? This feeling, she was greedy for it, perhaps starved for it, and most certainly didn't want to let it go.

Somehow, she made her way to the staircase that led up to the second floor. As she ascended, she glanced over to the garçonnière and noted a light still on in one of the second-story windows. She wondered distractedly if her father was still awake. It seemed a late hour for him. She was sure that it was approaching midnight.

Glancing down into the courtyard below, she saw the handsome cab was leaving, and Benjamin and Jack were still conversing. As if in response to her stare, Jack looked up, watching her, more than that, as though entirely focused on her. It felt strange, somehow as though she could still feel his hands touching her. She looked away with confusion, quickly opening the door that led inside.

❉

Jack waited in the courtyard for a moment, watching as Benjamin locked the gate to the carriageway and then returned to the courtyard. He breathed in the cool night air, steadying himself internally. Things tended to come in waves here, waves of quiet, stillness, and then bursts of unexpected activity. Sometimes the doors to traveling were open, using the powerful energy bands of the earth where his house was built, and sometimes not.

It could be predicted using astronomy if one studied the stars, but it was also something that you could feel, feel on your very skin if you are attuned.

The weeks following his marriage to Emma had been quiet, calm, in fact, unusually so. He'd been expecting memories to stir within his bride, memories of that night when she traveled and experienced things that she had not yet pieced together. But it did not seem to happen. She didn't even express a glimmer of that to him, nothing but stillness.

In some ways, he was grateful. It gave her time to adjust to her new circumstance without, well, other less-than-ordinary complications. But it had also left them both in a curious state of stasis, stuck in some respects in a place where they did not belong, unable to move over a peculiar sort of rift to where they should be.

And essentially, he wasn't a patient man, although he could fake it quite competently for a short duration. But this, this stretch, was becoming maddening for him.

He had no idea how torturous it would be for him to have Emma as his wife and not have Emma as his wife. So many times, he'd thought to use that private entrance between their rooms in the darkness of the night and join her in her bed. But he hadn't. He'd waited because, and he sighed deeply because he knew it wasn't time yet. But tonight — and then, the thought had floated off somewhere along the cool evening breeze.

He stood silently in the courtyard. Only the night sounds of the cicadas in the nearby trees were humming about him.

He needed to make a decision. Taking his lovely wife to the French Opera House had changed something within him. He had delighted in her company and her abandoned enjoyment of the evening. She seemed so different, so unguarded, much more like the Emma from a possible future he had met in his house years ago. Watching her, touching her, and kissing her, he'd become drunk with it, and he wanted, no, needed, more.

He stretched his feelings out. He could sense it, feel her pacing the wooden floor of the parlor above. She was waiting for him, nervous but more than that, curious.

He took a deep breath and headed upstairs. He'd decided. It was most definitely time to ignite the cycle of activity.

⚜

She'd almost left. If she retired now, he would probably leave her undisturbed, she thought. But then again, there was the dress. She wasn't at all sure she could unbutton it and unhook it without help. And Mattie had retired long ago. But if she asked for his help, Jack's help. Her breath quickened as she remembered the ride home.

The kisses they'd shared were even more intense, and then she stopped. She had memories somewhere of him kissing her in the same way, intensely, passionately. But it was jumbled. She wasn't sure when, when, and where that had occurred.

The noise of the door opening in the hallway startled her. Perhaps she should have retired. Things felt entirely too confusing at the moment.

As he walked into the parlor, she pulled her shawl more tightly around her shoulders. She was standing in front of the fireplace, but it wasn't lit tonight, and the chill of the room suddenly wrapped around her.

He stopped in the doorway, staring at her oddly, not exactly warmly, not exactly distantly, just sort of contemplative.

"Are you cold?" he asked softly.

"Yes, just a bit."

He nodded, heading to the table and pouring out a glass of brandy. "I'm sorry. I should have asked Benjamin to light the fire in here. I could do it myself if you like."

"No, it's not that bad," she murmured.

"Do you want something to drink?" His back was to her.

"No, no, I'm fine."

He turned around, his glass in hand. "Are you sure, Emma?"

She smiled hesitantly. Why did this feel so strange, so different? They'd had so many conversations since they married, but now it felt awkward, the air filled with, well, something. But then again, the whole evening had seemed, and she hesitated, trying to find a word that was adequate —transforming. "No, I'm all right, Jack. I just wanted to thank you for tonight," and then she glanced away. "The opera, it was lovely. I've never seen one before, but I enjoyed myself so very much."

He took a sip of brandy and then slowly placed it on the table beside him. "That pleases me to hear, Emma. As I said tonight, I truly want to make you happy."

She felt something in the timbre of his voice, something that told her he was indeed speaking the truth. "And what about your happiness, Jack? Does this arrangement truly make you happy?"

She didn't know why she'd asked the question except that it was truly something she wanted to know. But perhaps she shouldn't have. It certainly wasn't safe in any regard. He walked toward her. She thought to step back but was already near the brick wall beside the fireplace.

Then he was standing directly in front of her, so close, and it made her think of the feel of his arm around her, his hands on her waist, lifting her from the carriage to the ground.

He looked at her, searching, as though trying to puzzle her out. "What do you mean?" He said softly, although with a deep, insistent quality in his voice.

"I mean," she hesitated, "that I know you've done this to protect my father, marry me. And you've been so kind to me, Jack, but I wonder if that is really enough for you."

And then, quite suddenly, his hands were gently holding her arms, pulling her so much closer to him. "You don't believe that I care for you, Emma."

He was so near that she felt his breath, warm, laced with brandy. She was becoming besotted, and it wouldn't do, especially if— "How could you possibly, Jack? You scarcely know me. I was simply a means to an end," she said haltingly. She felt as though she was rambling, thoughts tumbling out unguarded into speech. But it was dizzying, his being so close. She could feel that undeniably powerful pull between them that felt so oddly unchecked tonight.

He took a sharp breath. And then she felt his hand caressing the side of her face. "Do you truly think that it wasn't you that I wanted, Emma? That it isn't you that I desperately want now?" And then, in the suddenness of an instant, he brought his mouth down onto hers, literally stealing her breath away. He folded her into his arms completely, effectively driving any doubts, or any thoughts for that matter, right out of her mind.

Chapter 24

The Turn

It was all energy, or at least that was the conclusion he'd come to over the past decade of study. The eternal spark or spirit, as he'd come to know, is fueled by energy. It is all connected: the physical self, emotional makeup, and spiritual well-being. All physical matter, at its core, is tied to the spiritual through energy. And within that reality lives the true treasure — the control and manifestation of energy.

"I still don't understand Mrs. Godfrey."

Nathaniel looked up from his desk, eyeing a much younger Jack with a renewed degree of focus. "It's difficult to reconcile the physical world we perceive with the true spiritual realm we all operate within."

Jack's head was spinning a bit. He had to admit that he was still a young man with the accompanying lustful appetites. The thought of venturing into a liaison just now for the sake of his physical needs appealed to him.

"You know the Templars took vows of chastity for a reason, young man. They understood the dangers of creating unwanted spiritual bonds and the havoc they could cause. Of course, for men, actual danger to the spirit only occurs with many liaisons, but with the woman, well, it's different. They have to be protected."

He frowned. Sometimes the information from Nathaniel came out in trickles. He plopped himself down on the sofa facing the old man's desk. "Elaborate," he stated flatly. He simply had no patience tonight.

"Women are more vulnerable in terms of energy. Their ability to give birth and have life created within their bodies also makes them powerful. But in the wrong relationship, their spirit can be damaged quite easily. That is why the marriage ceremony is so essential. It protects the participants, no draining, no damage, regardless of the nature of the union."

He sighed deeply, "So, Mrs. Godfrey?"

"Was a drainer, my boy. It's a rung of spiritual evolvement. The spirit is looking to evolve, so it pulls energy from others who are vulnerable. We've all been there in some past life. We have to learn not to do so."

"But you are implying our liaison could have spiritually damaged her."

"So, she pulls more energy from these bonds to protect and repair herself."

"You must admit all of this sounds so nefarious, Nathaniel."

He laughed shortly, "Well, it's all quite unconscious, my boy. It's difficult for a drainer to settle into their real-life path here on earth. They're always constantly drawn this way and that by a shiny new bauble, one to drain from. It gets distracting."

Jack understood. He didn't want to understand, but he did. Unfortunately, it looked like his life course just now was to be some sort of monk.

"But you married, Nathaniel."

The old man looked at him oddly. He leaned back in his chair. "Just as these are unsuitable matches, there are good ones as well. Lizette and I didn't have much time together, but our union was good. You'll also find someone, and all that is negative in a bad match will be quite turned around."

✣

Of course, he had known it even before they'd actually physically met, and again that evening on the riverboat dock when he'd touched her hand. He could feel it — the energy once their skin touched. It was something chemical, atoms, and ions colliding, sparking, and each time the pull increasing.

What Nathaniel had failed to tell him was that once the connection was stirred, the intoxication, dare he say, addiction of a sort followed. His mind told him to use caution, slow down with Emma, but tonight something had shifted, ostensibly had possessed him, and he couldn't stop or perhaps wouldn't.

He felt her trembling in his arms, but not from fear. He felt her emotions seeping into her skin. For him, it was impossible not to tangibly feel that she trembled with repressed, turbulent desire building up inside her, a desire she battled against. A desire that he knew instinctively she'd wearied of repressing.

He readjusted his embrace around her and picked her up off the ground. His head, his body, pounded with need, overwhelming hunger. He'd managed to make her his wife legally. Now he would do so physically, emotionally, and spiritually.

"Jack," she murmured with some muffled concern in her voice.

With a determined but rapid pace, he strode with her down the hallway toward his bedroom, Emma still tucked snugly in his arms. "It's all right," he soothed. She was still afraid, but he would manage all of this.

He pushed the bedroom door shut behind him with his foot. And then lightly placed his wife on the bed, their bed now, or so he believed. She looked at him with eyes wide but clearly glazed with passion. He removed his tuxedo jacket, threw it onto a nearby chair, and undid his tie. She watched silently, eyes so luminous and green.

And then he leaned over her, kissing her mouth again, and feeling her arms tentatively go around him, pulling him closer.

His hands moved down her dress, then he got up, pulling her up with him. His fingers went to the buttons at her back quickly as he unfastened them.

✤

It was dizzying, confusing, all of it. She couldn't think. She couldn't stop Jack and wasn't sure she wanted to. She was his wife, and she knew sooner or later he would want to claim his marital rights. But that cold statement of fact and what was happening now felt so far afield.

She was breathing deeply as she felt his hands on her skin, pulling down the bodice of her dress, and his lips on her shoulders as he deftly continued to pull her clothing away.

"Emma, love," he murmured as he unlaced the stays of the corset beneath her gown.

Her head fell back as she felt his lips on hers, her neck, and he was simply touching her everywhere and then everywhere with his mouth. She felt helpless, overcome with wild emotions and an ache, a need deep within. "Jack," she murmured softly, repeatedly.

But he wasn't answering.

Then he stopped, and she knew somewhere in the back of her mind that he was taking off the rest of his clothing.

She watched him, just lying in front of him, completely nude. There were no thoughts of modesty or covering up because they were caught up in this other reality, this hypnotic haze.

And then he was lying next to her, pulling her body against his, flesh, skin meeting skin, such warmth. She moved against him and heard herself moaning, though it didn't sound like her at all.

Then he rolled her onto her back and continued to kiss her softly as he made love to her. "Emma, it's all right, Emma," and she freely relinquished all control to him.

✤

The dreams came freely, wrapping around her with comfort. She walked through the silent, imposing hallways of Belle Coeur. Her aunt and cousins had left on a day trip to visit relatives in Plaquemine Parish. And as was so often the case, Emmeline was left behind. The servants of the great house had taken this opportunity to either leave to look after their own affairs or retreat to their rooms downstairs to rest.

So, as it was, Emmeline felt virtually alone. Her footsteps seemed to echo through the long hallway, cutting through the enveloping silence. It wasn't as though she minded being alone. It allowed her to relax and be herself, to be that young girl filled with curiosity and imagination — the one she kept hidden away, rolled up in her stern exterior. In some ways, it was just like the knights of the old days with their shiny metal armor designed to protect her from every outward blow. And for her, the emotional blows had always been the most damaging.

"You're unwanted."

"You're odd."

"You don't belong here."

The La Maire girls, at times, unleashed these ugly weapons against her. Of course, her aunt had implicitly permitted them to do so. Otherwise, Emmeline was sure they wouldn't have transgressed so far on their own. So, in defense, she had erected her special protection, deflecting those blows. If one were indifferent, it wouldn't hurt — such toxic barbs. She'd achieved this, and she was only twelve.

She took the grand mahogany staircase quietly up to the second floor. There was a lovely stretch of corridor just past the landing with old ancestral portraits. Often, she would whisper to them and imagine that they replied.

As she distractedly turned the corner, she stopped sharply, jolted roughly out of her quiet reverie. She wasn't expecting to see anyone, but a young man stood at the end of that grand hallway. Definitely older than she, but young, just the same, he wasn't dressed up, just a loose-fitting jacket, pants, and a shirt. To be truthful, she thought he looked a bit rumpled. Perhaps he was the son of one of the servants, but then again, she truly had never seen him before.

She walked a little closer, not anticipating any danger, although during her lifetime, there had never been much of anyone who warned her of potential dangers. That would denote caring, and no one, barring a few exceptions, cared for her much.

"I am more than certain you shouldn't be here," she delivered quite crisply for a twelve-year-old.

She stopped halfway down the great corridor while he remained in his original spot. He was blonde, quite blondish, hair a little longer than most of the men she'd seen, and in truth, that had not been many.

She frowned. She didn't like being ignored. "Did you hear me?"

"I did," he spoke, sort of blandly or rather with nothing distinguishable in his speech.

She took another step toward him. Why she couldn't quite say, except that it seemed the thing to do. "Then why are you here?"

He frowned. She saw him frown at her. Why was that? "You're very young," he said.

Her eyes widened. That bothered her. Why again, exactly, she couldn't say. "I'm twelve, not that it's your business. And why didn't you answer my question? My aunt won't like the idea of a stranger walking through her house."

"I thought she left you."

The sharp intake of breath pierced right through her armor of indifference, "Just for the day, they all went out."

"Everyone except you."

Now was her turn to frown, again, and how did he know all this? He was the stranger. "You know that's rude to say that. That isn't my fault."

"I know Emma. None of it is your fault."

Had she moved closer? She was now standing in front of him, the stranger who seemed familiar. "You know my name," although it wasn't exactly right, at this moment, it oddly felt as though it were.

"Yes, you're Emma, and I am James. I came here to tell you to hold on. That one day, things will be better for you. You will be out of this place. I promise."

"How can you know that? And why would I want to leave?" she whispered. She couldn't feel her armor at all now. Where had it gone?

Strangely, he looked at her as though he didn't believe her. "Surely, you're not happy here. Not in this place. It still carries the suffering and darkness as all these plantation houses do."

She thought to retort sharply, then she considered his words for a moment. He must mean the slaves. It had been quite a few years since the war, and all of that had changed. But it was true that when she walked about the great house, particularly out near the fields where many of the workers still lived, she still felt it at times, that heavy pressure in her chest as though she couldn't breathe. And at night, there were the shadows that in her nightmares would gather all around these halls like a swarm. "So, you do understand," he said, almost in response to her thoughts.

"Yes, maybe," she replied with trepidation. "But I don't understand who you are or why you think you know things about me."

"Because one day in the future, I'll be your husband."

Now she frowned, even more of a frown than before. "That's not true. I'll never marry, and I'll tell my aunt you were here."

"Yes, you will marry, and you'll marry me. But you won't remember any of this."

And then, her eyes snapped open.

Chapter 25

Pieces

The room was largely cast in shadows, though a faint glow from the hurricane lamp in the hallway slipped beneath the space at the bottom of the closed door. It took her some moments to connect with where she was. It wasn't her room, although her nightgown was draped across a nearby chair. The bed was larger, the bedspread a velvety dark brown shade. As she moved, she felt the sheets and quilt atop her brush her bare skin.

She'd been sleeping so deeply that waking up was very disorienting. She glanced beside her, and it filtered in thoroughly that, indeed, this wasn't her bed, and Jack was asleep next to her, lying on his back in the same disrobed state she found herself in.

Flashes of the night before rushed in, vivid, sensual detail, hypnotic in their intensity. Had that really happened? Had her husband and she made passionate love last night in this very bed? Or was that recollection the dream? The ache, soreness she felt between her legs attested to the fact that this was all too real.

She shifted beneath the covers again, and a deep voice emanated from what she thought previously was the sleeping man beside her. "Are you cold?" he said softly. "I brought your nightgown in from your room after you fell asleep."

It felt a bit startling to confront this intimacy so quickly. "I'm all right," she murmured, pulling the covers up more tightly beneath her chin.

He turned on his side, facing her, and she remembered last night running her hands along the muscles of that very same chest.

"Were you dreaming?" he asked.

"Yes," she said quietly. Then she felt his hand lightly touching her cheek. "You should rest," he murmured. And she closed her eyes, having no idea what to say.

❧

There was a soft knock at the door, and her eyes flickered open, adjusting to the brightness of the unfamiliar bedroom. Again, a gentle knock but ever so persistent. She sat up in the bed, pulling the covers up with her.

Then it filtered in that the space beside her was empty. "Yes," she answered, her voice sounding a little hoarse in her ears.

"It's Mattie, ma'am, with your morning tea."

"One moment," she said, spying her cotton nightgown. Moving rather quickly, she pulled it over her head and settled back beneath the covers. "All right, Mattie," she answered a bit shakily.

Her young maidservant pushed into the doorway, smiling, and opened the door, coming in with her usual tray — a cup of tea and a biscuit. They'd settled into this routine sometime after she moved into her father's house. Emma had not taken breakfast with her father, nor, more recently, her husband. Instead, Mattie would bring her a hot cup of tea in the morning with a single biscuit with one pat of butter on it. But today, instead of bringing it to Emma's usual room, she was now bringing it to Dr. Fallon's private quarters.

Mattie greeted her with a smile, not betraying in the least any reaction to her change of circumstance. She set the cherry wood tray down on a nearby bedside table. "Dr. Jack said that you might be sleeping a bit later this morning, so I didn't bring this as early as I usually do."

She nodded, feeling a bit of a flush run rampant up her cheeks, "That's fine, thank you, Mattie."

She started toward the door, then paused a moment. "Oh, Dr. Jack said you might be wanting your things moved into this room today. I can see to that later if you like."

The breath sort of fled her chest a bit at the comment. He certainly didn't waste any time. "I'll let you know about that later. Thank you, Mattie."

Something flickered in the young woman's eyes for a moment. Emma thought perhaps curiosity, but then it was muffled out by her calm demeanor. "Yes, ma'am," she said, quickly leaving the room and closing the door behind her. This was their usual routine. And in about half an hour, Mattie would return to see if Emma needed any help dressing for the day.

Her eyes drifted to her evening gown, carelessly strewn across the chair from last night. Jack must've picked it up this morning when he left. She'd slept so heavily that she hadn't even heard him leave.

She leaned back in the bed, her face flushing even more strongly at the memory of the night before. It had been so intense, unexpected in some ways, and yet, in others, completely natural. There had been no awkwardness, just an instinctual need for each other.

She sighed deeply. Everything was changing, headed in an unknown direction. And that, more than anything, frightened her intensely.

✻

Jack had already left for the hospital by the time she came downstairs. Mattie had returned and helped her dress, and Emma had put her off on the matter of moving her things to the main bedroom. She didn't want to consider any of that yet. In her mind, one night of intimacy did not make a marriage. But she felt oddly not herself, vulnerable somehow, as though some of that armor she'd erected so long ago had disintegrated, and an unexpected underbelly of emotion was now laid bare.

Around midmorning, after hours of contemplating unsettled emotions, she decided to visit her father. It had actually been several days since she'd seen him, then in the company of Jack. When they moved, she had no idea they would live so separate from him, although she knew that Jack spent time with him daily.

With a measure of determination, she crossed the courtyard, heading to the garçonnière and taking its staircase up to her father's quarters. Of course, she knew she would have to get past the lion at the gate, nurse Amelia Clay. But she believed Jack had spoken to her, causing a somewhat softening of her attitude toward Emma's access to her father. After all, he was her father, regardless of the fact that she scarcely knew him.

She knocked firmly on the double oak doors at the upstairs entrance. And they were opened slightly by the nurse in question.

"Oh, Mrs. Fallon," she said, looking genuinely surprised.

"Hello, Amelia. I've come to pay my father a visit."

Several emotions seem to flicker across the middle-aged woman's face — surprise, doubt, and confusion among them. "Oh, well, yes, Dr. Fallon did tell me that you would want to see Mr. Nathaniel more often."

"Yes, and I would like to see him now."

"Well, yes, ma'am. But I must warn you, Dr. Lescale seems out of sorts today, confused if I may say so," she said briskly.

"Yes, fine, Amelia, I stand warned. Now will you step aside so that I can come in?"

Emma could see that Amelia's face steeled a bit, but then she stepped back, opening the door further. "Of course, Ma'am."

The rooms in the garçonnière were all connected, with no hallways. A front sitting room led directly into her father's study, which connected to his bedroom, and another one beyond that evidently belonged to Amelia Clay. In addition, of course, there was the lavatory as well. And there were various other doors attaching the rooms in ways she was unaware of. Apparently, it was the old Creole style of house design, one that had not been emulated at Belle Coeur.

Her father's study that Jack had meticulously set up for him was kept tidy and bright — the shutters open and plenty of light flooding in. She couldn't fault Amelia. She did appear to be taking excellent care of Nathaniel.

Not unexpectedly, he sat behind his desk, wearing his reading glasses, and examining a very large book that appeared to be handwritten upon closer inspection. She stood in the center of the room for some moments as Amelia had opted not to join her in the study. Once she realized that he would not acknowledge her without a bit of prodding, she said loudly, "Nathaniel," again, never actually feeling comfortable addressing him as father.

The old man suddenly looked up, as though for the first time, realizing there was someone else in the room with him. He stood up from his chair rather abruptly, pulling off his glasses and greeting her with a tremendous smile. "Lizette," he whispered with an animation in his voice that truly she had never heard before.

Emma's stomach clutched a bit in anxiety. Amelia had said that he was confused today. "No," she said a bit forcefully, as this was more than a bit disturbing to her to be called by her deceased mother's name. "It's Emma, your daughter."

"Daughter?" He said blankly. "Why are you sporting with me, Lizette? I have no daughter."

"Yes, you do, Nathaniel," she said a bit more firmly.

He frowned, looking displeased with her, but she preferred that to the lovesick adoration she'd seen in his eyes moments before. "No, no, my dear. It's that boy, playing around with your memories, making you think things that aren't true, making you forget other things. He's too good at it, you know, mesmerism. He wanted to help his patients, make them forget their pain. That's why he studied it, but he's too good at it."

Her head suddenly began to swirl at his bizarre ramblings, but even more so, something about this hit her uncomfortably as truth.

"What boy are you talking about?" she said shakily.

"The boy," he repeated emphatically, "Jack Fallon."

Chapter 26

Backsliding

She sat outside in the courtyard for a while, for quite some time, just thinking, actually feeling completely drained. It was very cool today, but then again, she hadn't brought a shawl with her when she visited her father.

It hadn't been a long visit, but so disturbing and perhaps enlightening in some ways. It had continued in much the same vein, with him insisting that she was her dead mother and that Emma simply did not exist. And, of course, he was emphatic with the assertion that Jack, her new husband, whom she had given herself fully to the night before, was some sort of sorcerer and could control people's minds.

After several minutes of the building chaos, Amelia had poked her head in, declaring that it was time for Mr. Nathaniel's medicine. She hadn't met the nurse's eyes. She didn't want her to know what this visit had done to her, what in some respects it had cost her. Instead, Emma had taken the opportunity for a hasty exit.

And here she sat, a chapping wind blowing through the courtyard, but she couldn't muster the energy to go inside, get a shawl, or do much of anything.

In fact, for some reason that was not wholly inexplicable, she couldn't seem to move. This, all of it, must be nonsense. After all, Jack had said that Nathaniel's mind was deteriorating, and here was clear evidence of it. He'd insisted repeatedly that she was his dead wife. Of course, everyone had always spoken of her resemblance to Lizette Charbonnet, but for him to mistake the two of them. What further evidence did she need of his infirmity?

But still, his words, how they nagged at her. *"It's that boy, playing around with your memories, making you think things that aren't true, making you forget other things."*

It felt like a stab in her heart. It was true that she did feel confused about things, events, and had been so since before the wedding. Flashes, snatches of images would flow through her mind. But then she rejected them as imaginings, fancifulness.

"You see, thoughts are actually energy forms. If you focus, it is much easier to intercept their import." His voice, Jack's. Had he said that, or did she imagine it?

Her stomach clutched with queasiness. She wondered if she, too, was losing her mind like her father, entertaining such possibilities. Or, as bad as that seemed, was it much worse?

She rose and walked slowly, pacing across the courtyard, trying to focus. The wedding, the days leading up to the wedding, she'd always been intent on not getting married. But then she had. She married Jack Fallon, though somewhere in the back of her mind, she'd been set against it.

She grabbed hold of the back of one of the patio's cast-iron chairs to steady herself. Was it possible that he'd somehow influenced her thoughts as her father claimed he could do? Was all of this, all of it, Jack's contrivance?

✳

He hadn't intended to be gone all day from the house, but complications with one of his patients at the Hotel Dieu demanded his attention until almost early evening. As his carriage headed down Bienville Street, he felt an inexplicable wave of anxiety pass over him. It didn't make sense. He should feel nothing but optimism about his future with Emma after the night they'd shared together. Their union was no longer in name only. It had been consummated, and they had connected on levels that, in time, would begin to unfold themselves. This morning he'd thought to wake her as he was leaving the house, but she had been sleeping so soundly that he opted instead not to disturb her.

But as he led the rig down the carriageway and into the courtyard, a more profound tremor of concern traveled across his spine. It was a foreshadowing of something near, some taint to their newfound happiness. As he gave the reins over to Benjamin, who had met him in the dusky courtyard, Amelia Clay approached them from the staircase of the garçonnière . "I was wondering, Dr. Fallon, if I might take a moment of your time." He nodded, pausing momentarily as Benjamin disappeared into the stables with the horse and carriage.

"Yes, Amelia, what is it?" He asked, marking the concern on her face.

"Well, Doctor, I know you told me to be more liberal with my access to Mr. Nathaniel, I mean, concerning Mrs. Fallon."

His eyes drifted beyond her to the upstairs of his home. For a moment, he thought he saw the drapes flutter in Emma's old window, and then again, perhaps not. "Yes, that's right, Amelia."

"Yes, sir, well, Mrs. Fallon did pay a visit to her father this morning. And while I did not hear the conversation, at one point, I heard voices raised in upset of some kind."

He focused solely on Amelia's face, wondering if it was indeed true that she did not hear the details of the conversation. "Go on," he said sternly.

"Well, when I went in to see what it was all about, I saw that Mr. Nathaniel was very agitated. He was having one of his bad spells, Dr. Fallon. And I told Mrs. Fallon that before she went to see him, but she insisted."

"I see," he said under his breath.

"Yes, sir, well, Mr. Nathaniel was being very loud, calling your wife Lizette or something like that, and Mrs. Fallon was very pale, sir. And she said nothing but just quickly left the room."

"Is Nathaniel all right?"

"Yes, sir, I gave him something to calm him. But I haven't seen Mrs. Fallon since."

He nodded, lost in thought. Clearly, all of this was connected to those foreboding premonitions that he had experienced on his way home. "Thank you, Amelia. Please keep me updated on my father-in-law's condition."

"Oh yes, sir," and she turned, walking briskly back to the garçonnière.

Pensively, he headed into the downstairs entrance of the townhouse. As he entered the dining room, he was almost immediately greeted by Mattie.

"Oh, Dr. Fallon, Hilda can fix your dinner whenever you wish. Miss Emma wanted me to tell you she isn't feeling well tonight and won't be joining you."

He sighed inwardly as more pieces began to fall together. "All right, Mattie. I think I'd like to check on Emma. Then I'll let you know my plans."

She smiled nervously as she left. Clearly, Mrs. Clay wasn't the only one who had picked up on the realization that something was amiss.

He bounded up the steps to the second floor, heading toward his bedroom. As he opened the closed door, he hoped rather than believed that he would find Emma tucked away in the large cherry wood bed. But his heart sank a bit to find it empty.

Distracted, he laid his hat and coat on a chair. Evidently, whatever positive footing he'd felt they were on since last night had been undermined sometime during his absence. Well, no matter. He was never one to shirk from a challenge. He placed his hand on the adjoining door and opened it.

The room was cast in shadows, and he could make out Emma's sleeping form in the bed if indeed she was asleep.

Without hesitation, he ignited the oil lamp on the dresser, illuminating the room.

She shifted in the bed. He noted her day dress on a nearby chair, and he saw as she moved that she was only clothed in a shift.

"Emma," he said quietly. "I want to talk to you."

Her hand went over her eyes as she moved beneath the covers. "Jack, I wasn't feeling well. I just wanted to go to sleep early."

He sat in a chair near the side of the bed. "Is it another headache?"

"No," she murmured. "I'm just tired."

"Have you eaten?"

"No, I wasn't hungry."

"Well, I want to talk to you. So, I'll have Mattie send a tray up to the parlor. Put on a robe and meet me there," he said a bit sternly. And then he stood up and left the room, closing the adjoining door behind him. Emma sat up in the bed, feeling quite jarred by his abrupt exit. She wasn't at all ready for this. She needed time to process things, but it seemed as though that wouldn't be happening tonight.

⚜

She pulled on a velvet dressing gown of dark purple that Pauline had given her last Christmas. It wasn't really very late, just after eight o'clock, but she had hoped to avoid, well, just everything, for the evening and hopefully most of tomorrow. As she entered the parlor, she noted that Mattie had already left a covered tray on Jack's desk and two glasses of wine poured next to it. She'd taken her time getting up and dressing her hair a bit, time that she hoped would help her put things in order, at least in her mind. She wasn't ready, not nearly ready to confront Jack about the circumstances she questioned, the things she suspected. But unfortunately, it seemed her new husband was not content to give her time to dodge this particular confrontation. Of course, she could wait, not bring it up, but then that choice would also supply its own challenges.

When she entered the parlor, she saw that he was facing the window overlooking the street below, clearly lost in thought.

"You should have eaten without me. I told Mattie that I wasn't hungry," she said softly.

He turned around, seeming a bit surprised at her silent entrance. "Yes, I know that's what you said. Won't you sit for a while?" he replied, indicating the sofa. She sat down, aware that he was watching her, watching all her movements with great interest. Once settled, she looked up into his intense gaze. "Are you ill, Emma?" He asked.

"No, not really," she answered calmly.

He crossed the room to sit beside her on the sofa. "But something is bothering you."

She swallowed, wondering again if, indeed, now was the time to bring up any of this. "I'm out of sorts. That's all. There have been a lot of changes quickly."

Seamlessly, he took her hand in his, pressing it softly. "You must tell me how I can help."

She breathed in sharply. It bothered her, all the emotions that she felt bubbling up inside her. "Honestly, you could tell me the truth, Jack."

She glanced up, seeing a bit of surprise in his expression. "The truth? Do you think I've been deceptive in some way?"

"I don't know. Have you been, Jack Fallon?"

His eyes widened somewhat, and then he withdrew his hand. "Mrs. Clay told me that you visited Nathaniel today."

"Yes," she replied succinctly.

"And did he say something that made you doubt me?"

She inhaled sharply, trying to figure out exactly how to launch into this. "Well, he did seem confused. He called me Lizette, my mother's name."

"Yes, I did tell you his mental state was unstable."

"Of course, but he also talked about you. He said that you must have influenced my memories. That you have the power of mesmerism," she said, staring at him directly.

"And that's why you didn't want to see me this evening, Emma? You believe the rantings of a disturbed man."

She stood up abruptly, walking away from him. Her mind swirled a bit with confusion and the intense pressure of the moment. "I don't know, Jack. What I do know is there are things I can't remember clearly about being here, and the time leading up to the wedding feels as though there was a heavy fog over my mind. Is it possible, Jack? Please tell me the truth. Did you somehow influence me?"

"A mesmerist does not have the power to make someone do something against their will," he said firmly.

"That's not what I asked," she flung back at him. "I asked you if it is true that you have such abilities?"

He stood up slowly, staring at her with an odd expression. "Nathaniel is right. I do."

Again, that sensation that was becoming oddly familiar to her, the one that felt as though the ground was indeed shifting beneath her feet. "What?" She whispered in disbelief. "And did you —"

"Influence you to accept the marriage? Yes, I did. But as I said, I could not make you do something you were dead set against."

It was dizzying, unreal, hearing the admission coming from him, so direct, so unflinching. "All of this because of my father?"

He moved quickly to her, taking the sides of her arms into his hands. "No, of course not, Emma. I wanted you, knew we needed to be together."

"And you could not let me choose that for myself?" She barely got out.

There was something in his eyes, indecision, pain perhaps. "I'm sorry. I did what I thought was best. Things were escalating too quickly with Nathaniel and other events." His voice dropped off, but images flooded across her mind — a man with a pale face, and a thing, a creature right here in the parlor.

She stepped back, violently pulling away from him. "You shouldn't have lied to me."

His face hardened a bit. "There was no influence last night, Emma. That was your choice."

It took the breath out of her, his reference to their intense intimacy the night before. "Maybe I didn't feel as though I had a choice. That I was compelled to make this marriage work."

He smiled, stepping forward and lightly touching her cheek with his fingertips. "I felt you in my arms, Emma. You can't tell me that was just complacency. Don't lie to yourself."

Again, she pulled away, "Stop it. I won't have you control me."

She turned, heading down the hallway and through the door to the outside. She had to get some air to think clearly. In the semidarkness, she headed down the staircase to the courtyard when a somewhat familiar and yet unyielding rush of dizziness began to overtake her.

Chapter 27

An Uneasy Truce

As the dizziness threatened to sweep in on her, Emma focused intently, using her anger and determination to ground her to this moment. She flew down the staircase into the courtyard below, stalking to its outer perimeter, then stopping. Behind her, she heard what she assumed were her husband's quick footsteps following.

"I don't want to talk to you anymore. I've decided to leave, to go home to Belle Coeur."

There was silence for a moment, and then finally, "You can't go back," he said firmly.

She turned around slowly, staring through the shadows. Jack was standing motionless some feet away from her. "What do you mean?"

"This is good," he murmured distractedly. "You've managed to anchor yourself here."

"Anchor myself?" she asked, then suddenly she understood. "You were afraid I'd be—"

"Yes, traveling again."

She crossed her arms in front of her, entirely vulnerable in this awkward moment. "Then it was all true, those memories, the ghost, the creatures, people, even you, but from other times."

"Yes, of course, all true I'm afraid. Nathaniel and I have been doing this for years."

She shook her head emphatically, "I want no part of it, Jack. No more of this."

He nodded slowly, "I see why you would believe that after what I've done. I am sorry all of this has been so upsetting for you. It's not how I wanted things to be. But it's really all too late. There just is no going back. You see, a side effect of traveling is that you begin to see things as they truly are. Belle Coeur is not home to you. It's a terrible place, tainted by the sins committed there, dark with an infection that is impossible to heal."

His words chilled her as the distant memory of its halls filled with shadows overcame her, a memory of dark, unseen serpents slithering down the great staircase of that grand old house. "I-I don't understand what you mean," she stumbled across her words as more images seeped into her memory, images of nightmares from so long ago.

And then he walked closer, out of the darkness, until he was standing right in front of her. "The problem isn't that you don't understand. The problem is that you most certainly do. Everything has an energy, and every action has a consequence. People were enslaved on that plantation. They were abused and tortured, and all of that leaves an imprint, a negative energy that draws darkness and degrades light. And sometimes gives birth to abominations."

More images were flashing across her mind, images of those creatures in the parlor of the house when she and Jack were traveling that night so long ago. "Those things we saw. You said back then that they were looking to feed, were parasites."

"Yes, of course, our world is littered with such insects, parasites. Some seen, others not."

"And Belle Coeur?"

"Infested, of course, with all manner of creatures that such a magnitude of negativity invites."

She took in a deep, horrified breath. "I don't know if I can believe you."

"You don't have to. You can feel it now, Emma. See it, if you focus with your mind. Your sensitivities have expanded."

She frowned, now suddenly feeling a tug, a powerful pull, as if she just let go now, she would indeed be elsewhere.

"Resist it," he said quickly. "Anchor yourself here. It wouldn't do to travel in your present state of mind. You're upset and might end up in dark places."

"Dark places?" she repeated hesitantly.

"Energy attracts," he said, whispering to her as he was so close to her now, so close he could easily reach out and touch her. "Low emotions, anger, sadness, and upset draw negativity."

And then she felt him, ever so lightly caressing her face with his fingertips. "You need to be calm."

"I-I don't know what to do now, what I should do," she murmured with upset.

And then, lightly, he turned her face toward him and softly began to kiss her. "Jack, don't," she whispered. But it felt so calming to her just allowing it. "I can't trust you," she whispered as he pulled her against him.

"You can, Emma. Let me help now," he said softly as he continued to hold and kiss her beneath the moonlight.

✤

It would have been so easy for him to draw her right back into the intimacy they'd shared the night before. But when the harsh light of day crept in, she would hate him for it. So instead, Jack opted for comfort as he guided her back up the stairs and toward their bedroom. His arm was around her, and rather than trying to influence her in any way, he was giving her energy through the contact. It was something that seemed to be quite natural between them.

He could feel the confusion and tumultuous emotions racing through his wife. Her mind was in conflict while her essence and her body reached out to him for solace.

"Jack, I need time to think. I can't just forget what's happened."

"I know," he murmured as he led her into the bedroom. "We're going to rest like we did when we were at The Magnolia Hotel in Biloxi."

"I should go back to my room," she whispered. But then he bent down and softly kissed her again, slowly unbuttoning her dressing gown.

"Not tonight, let me hold you," he said softly.

She allowed him to do so, conflicted as she was. Sitting on the edge of the bed, she looked at him with wide eyes, reminding him so much of that young girl he'd encountered in his astral travels to Belle Coeur so long ago. Without protest, she allowed him to pull off her dressing gown, leaving the plain shift she wore beneath.

And then he stepped back and began to undress himself, taking off his shirt and pants as she watched soundlessly, then reaching into his bureau for a nightshirt to put on. After methodically turning off the oil lamps he moved to the other side of the bed. Fluidly, he reached over, pulling Emma beneath the covers with him and into his arms. Again, he kissed her deeply, more passionately than he should. And he felt her respond despite what had occurred between them.

"We'll talk more tomorrow," he said in the darkness, holding her closely until, after some time, he felt her drift off to sleep.

❀

"You have to be careful here."

"Why do you say that?" she'd asked.

He looked at her strangely, but for some reason, his eyes seemed much older and wiser than they should at his young age. *"Because there are monsters here."*

She frowned, *"What kind of monsters?"*

"The shadow kind."

She sat up in the bed with a jolt. Beside her, Jack was still sleeping. She looked to the partially drawn curtains and saw that outside it was still night. But it felt as though there was an intense pressure in her heart.

"What is it, Emma?" He said beside her through the darkness.

She put her hand on her chest, trying to draw in air. "I don't know. It's hard to breathe."

Suddenly, he was sitting up, pulling her against him, and placing his hand directly over her heart. "Focus on peace, Emma. Concentrate on a white light surrounding you."

She tried, but it was too difficult. She was panicked as though she was drowning in water. "I can't. I can't get air."

"It's all right, Emma. Try to be calm. Something is trying to attack you. Were you dreaming?"

"Yes, yes, I was back at Belle Coeur with someone."

"It's all right," he murmured, continuing to rub her heart area. "Something got hold, but it will pass. Focus on peace, my love."

She tried to relax but still felt the tremendous pressure. Shadows, all she could feel was shadows wrapping around her so tightly. Instinctively and in a panic, she turned in his arms, reaching up and pressing her mouth against his. She could feel him hesitate, then turn her around, drawing her body securely against his while returning the kiss. She could feel him begin to caress her, and wherever he touched seemed to ease the attacking pressure she was feeling.

There weren't words as he moved her seamlessly onto her back and lifted the gown away that she wore. His touch, his kisses, were all easing the attack she was feeling as everything between them merged into passion.

Chapter 28

Precarious Steps

Emma woke unsteadily to the morning light being filtered through the drapes. Lethargic, every inch of her felt absolutely sluggish as she tried to piece together where she was and what had happened. Flashes of the night before began to dribble in as she pulled herself up to a sitting position on the bed. She glanced at a nearby chair where both her deep purple dressing gown and white shift that she wore beneath it were draped.

She pulled the covers up higher. Of course, that was why she was feeling chilled. She really should, out of decency's sake, put something on. But she felt absolutely drained of energy, and with that, the inclination to do anything.

Well, she certainly put Jack Fallon in his place last night for his questionably bad behavior. Clearly, by the end of the evening, she ended up in his bed again, more than fulfilling her wifely obligations. What was it about that man that seemed to flip all her steadfast resolutions right on their head?

Of course, if she were being honest, and at the moment she had no wish to be, there was a whole lot that had happened in between that reflected a more nuanced light on the situation.

But she didn't care to be fair just now, just perhaps to feel better and have something warm to eat.

She forced herself to her feet, then took the few steps it would take to procure her dressing gown. Slipping it over her head, she didn't bother with the shift beneath, too much fatigue for such details. A bit languorously, she perched on the edge of the bed and began to button up the long purple robe. It felt soft against her bare skin beneath, curiously reminding her of her husband's hands that had caressed her to distraction the night before.

How in the world did she get here? A man who had admitted to her that he used some sort of mesmerism on her to get her to the altar was now her lover. And not a lover that was uninvited because for some unfathomable reason she'd felt desperate for him last night. There was an integral need inside her to be with this man.

She sighed deeply, having no idea what to make of any of this. Then the lightest tapping on the door interrupted her laborious deliberations.

"Who is it?" She called out, completely expecting an answer from Mattie.

"It's Jack, Emma."

There was no time for more pondering or drafting a new plan, it seemed. "Come in," she answered hesitantly.

And in seconds, her husband was inside the room, fully dressed for the day, closing the door behind him. She eyed him with curiosity. "What time is it?"

"It's one. You've slept most of the day."

It was true. She still felt a daunting lethargy clinging to her. "Well, I do seem to be making a habit out of this. I don't know what's wrong with me. I feel absolutely exhausted." And then she looked to him again, frowning. "You've been out."

"Yes," he was still staring at her with concern, "morning rounds at the hospitals, but I'm home this afternoon."

She nodded. "Regardless of what happened last night, between us. I am still angry, you know, upset about the marriage."

And then she hesitated, "I mean, about how it was accomplished."

"Yes, well," he said slowly, looking distracted, she would have to say. "Perhaps, in time, I will be forgiven." And then there was a slight smile. "If I work at it."

"You know, last night, Jack. It wasn't what I intended. I wanted more time to consider things, but then—"

"But then we ended up in bed together, re-consummating a marriage you're not sure you really want." He filled in abominably.

"Is that what we were doing?" she murmured.

And then he was sitting beside her, hand in hers. "I don't want you to be unhappy."

"I'm not. I am a bit confounded. So much I don't understand, you know."

And then he gently tipped her chin so that she was facing him. "Yes, and I'd like a chance to remedy some of that if you're willing. It's the weekend. Let's spend it together, and I will try to help you understand what's been happening."

She looked into his eyes, and they seemed earnest and sincere, but could she trust him? That indeed was another matter. "Yes, I think that is important if we want to move forward."

He smiled, then softly kissed her on the lips. Passion, how easily he could light that spark within her. In some ways, it was frightening because the control she'd spent the balance of her life forging was being eroded in the blink of an eye. "How about I get Mattie to send you up something to eat with a cup of tea?"

She nodded, "All right, Jack."

And then he patted her hand. "Give it a little time, Emma. I promise you'll feel better about things."

And she wondered with disquiet if that was a promise he could keep.

❋

Mattie seemed unusually quiet as she brought Emma a light soup and toast for lunch, as well as a hot cup of tea.

"Are you feeling better, Ma'am?" she asked tentatively as she came to clear the dishes and help Emma put on her day dress. It was gray, like so many of the other outfits she owned, and for the first time, well, possibly the first time, she considered replacing much of her wardrobe. "I think so, Mattie," she answered. And then she smiled at the young maid. "I do appreciate your concern."

Those few words seemed to cheer the young woman a bit. "Dr. Jack asked that you join him in the upstairs parlor once you were dressed.

"Yes," she murmured. "Thank you."

And at that, young Mattie quickly exited, leaving her again in her solitary contemplations.

It was confusing to her, trying to balance the chain of events in her mind and, in any way, evaluating the state of her marriage.

Culturally and legally, she supposed there weren't many options. She was wed to Jack Fallon. Like it or not, she was his wife. To change that was no easy task, and from what she'd witnessed, not a reality easily escaped. As she'd always observed, a widow was the most secure and independent female in society. And while Jack Fallon did vex her at times and even perhaps outrage her, she did have affection for him.

But was that enough? And was that truly all she really felt?

With a conflicted heart, she left the bedroom and headed toward the front parlor of the house. As she entered, she was again instantly struck by a bizarre collage of images from that night that now felt like so long ago, the night Jack Fallon had invited her and Nathaniel to his home for dinner. It was undeniably the evening that had ostensibly changed everything.

Her husband was waiting there, seated behind the mahogany desk near the front windows, immediately looking up once she entered the room. "Emma," standing, he held out his hand to her. Silently, she crossed the room and tentatively joined him. "How are you?"

"I'm feeling better," she said.
"You must sit with me. I have been considering things."

Chapter 29

Nathaniel's Choice

There were choices at hand. Always choices, always paths that can lead you down one road or another.

"But how can you be sure you're making the right one?"

He recalled voicing his concern some years ago over a late-night brandy with Nathaniel Lescale. They had returned from a meeting with The Society of Magnetism, once a highly visible organization composed largely of lawyers, businessmen, and, of course, physicians who followed and implemented the teachings of Franz Mesmer — namely the transference of energy between animate and inanimate objects. This body, which had strong ties to a similar one in France, had virtually gone extinct during the Civil War, then resurfaced afterwards as a clandestine group virtually invisible to the public. It was this now underground society that Lescale had introduced him to and that he and Nathaniel were now contemplating breaking ties with to pursue radical explorations on their own terms.

"The right choice?" Nathaniel had responded with his quick dark eyes. *"Well, you can't. You follow your mind, your heart, and let the fates take their spoils."*

He was younger at the time and remembered wondering if his mentor was a bit mad with ambition. *"That sounds reckless."*

"Sometimes reckless is the only option, my friend."

✤

"What does that mean exactly, considering?" She asked hesitantly.

He looked deeply into her eyes and her lovely face. She was pale, and there was evidence of strain around her eyes and shadows beneath, certainly not the appearance of a happy bride. It bothered him the toll all this was having on her. It certainly wasn't what he had intended.

"I think we should speak to your father now."

Emma looked at him with a bit of confusion. "I visited with him only yesterday, Jack."

He squeezed her hand. "Yes, of course I know. But that is not exactly what I mean. I'm afraid I am going to have to ask that you trust me for a bit."

And then her lovely eyes widened. It was true. He might as well ask for the moon. "Really? Trust, now, Jack?"

He nodded emphatically. "Yes, yes, I know no one deserves it less. But in the spirit of moving forward. I will ask for the impossible." Resolutely, he said, "I want you to keep holding my hand and focus on not letting go this time."

It took a moment, but somewhat begrudgingly, she replied, "All right."

"Now come with me."

✤

It was unsettling, and on a level, Emma did understand that they were not going to see Nathaniel in the garçonnière. This was something else. Again, her head felt dizzy, that very peculiar dizziness that seemed to happen whenever she was *traveling*, as her husband put it.

"Jack, what's happening?" she said as they moved down the long hallway leading to the outer staircase.

"It's all right, Emma. I want you to focus intently on just two things. Staying with me and finding your father, Nathaniel." As he opened the doorway leading to the outside, Emma felt an even more profound rush of dizziness accompanied by vibrant colors slashing across her mind so powerful that it felt distinctly as though she was caught in some overwhelming storm.

Desperately, she tried to maintain focus on Nathaniel and hold onto Jack in the same moment. But she could feel her hand slipping from his and a powerful grayness unrelentingly sweeping across everything.

"You took a chance, bringing her here, Jack. It was dangerous, reckless."

"I understand, Nathaniel, but it felt warranted. Emma needs this to understand."

She heard the voices swelling around her, but her eyes were closed. "Smelling salts?"

"No, let her adjust on her own. Don't force anything."

She could smell wood burning, and the scent of candles somewhere, soft vanilla scented. And then her eyes flickered open. The room was dimly lit, but she did recognize it. They were in the parlor again, the one they'd left only moments before. And standing next to her was Jack, his face filled with concern.

"Are you all right?" he murmured, lightly touching her forehead.

Slowly, with his arms supporting her, he helped her sit up from her reclining position on the brocade sofa. And across the room was her father, staring at her intently. "Nathaniel," she whispered.

And then he came closer, approached her with a deliberateness in his step that she had not seen in him lately. "Yes, my dear. It is I."

"What are you doing here?"

There was a hesitation, and then he smiled broadly in a way she had never seen before. "The question is not that one but rather what are the two of you doing here."

*

"This is too perilous, Nathaniel. Some places should not be traversed by mortal man."

"You mean like Orpheus in the underworld," he laughed, seemingly to himself.

"I know losing your wife was devastating to you, Nathaniel."

"No, Jack, what you don't understand is that I know she is still out there. No, not in the physical realm, but changed, transformed. And if we can reach other planes of existence, we can reach hers as well."

*

Nathaniel was standing there, in front of them, just as he'd always been but also somehow transformed — full of energy, eyes alight with intelligence, and more than that, curiosity.

Emma reached out shakily, putting her hand on Jack's arm. "Have we travelled, Jack? Is this what is happening?"

"You know it's dangerous to travel this deep, my boy," The thin, wiry man standing in front of them stated emphatically.

"Emma needs to understand things," Jack repeated sternly. It was so strange to see the old man like this again. His mind was clearly as sharp as a razor and as aware as when he first knew him.

His new wife, however, was silent as though stunned by what she was witnessing. "He's so different," she murmured. It was true. Even though they had exchanged few words, she could see the alteration in her father's demeanor.

"Yes, the truth is that most of his consciousness exists here."

She turned to him with some alarm. "What does that mean? Most of his consciousness?"

Nathaniel looked at Jack with a sudden measure of disapproval. "Was this truly necessary?"

And then Jack answered in the only way he could, "I've always done what you've required of me, Nathaniel. You took me in when I was alone, gave me a life, a profession, and, in some ways, now the woman I love. But this is about Emma, Emma gaining some peace of mind, some understanding."

She stood up suddenly, startling them both. "I want you to stop. Stop talking about me as though I can't think for myself." And then she turned toward her father, looking at him almost imploringly, "Explain this to me."

"Yes, yes, my dear. You have come this far. It is the least of what I can do." He reached behind him, grabbed the desk chair and dragged it in front of the two of them. "Please sit for a moment, Emma. I need to gather my thoughts. I must confess I never expected to have this particular conversation with you."

She glanced over to Jack as if to gain some reassurance, and he nodded silently. So, they both sat on the sofa and waited.

Nathaniel was silent for a moment as if trying to find a place to begin. And when he finally did, his voice sounded tentative. "When your mother died, Emma. I think I lost myself, my mind perhaps in part, unquestionably my heart. You see, I broke inside. I did not understand that such a connection, such a love, was possible, and then so abruptly, it was taken away. I thought at times to simply let myself die, so I could join Lizette, but it seemed as though that was not in my power to do so. So instead, I threw myself wholeheartedly into finding her again."

"Finding her?" Emma repeated haltingly.

"You see, my dear, while this earthly flesh, the physical dies, the soul, the divine spark, is eternal. I knew this, and my pragmatic mind refused to accept that I could not achieve reconnection."

Jack felt Emma reach out and unconsciously grab his hand as Nathaniel continued. "I studied voraciously, traveled when I could, learned the esoteric arts, and applied them to science as I knew it in the physical realm. And then I found a partner here in young James Fallon. We pursued so many avenues, most trails that grew cold, dead ends, but then magnetism, magnetism began to yield results."

"Magnetism? What does that mean?" She looked to Jack, eyes wide.

"Energy bands are another description, very instrumental in medicine, healing, and then—"

"Traveling," she filled in shakily.

"Yes, traveling," Nathaniel repeated. "Jack and I found it to be the most viable avenue."

"For reconnecting with my dead mother?" Emma stated with some alarm.

"You must understand and accept my dear. Death is not the end of things. In most circumstances, it is the beginning. I always felt Lizette around me, saw her in my dreams, and heard her voice whispering to me at times. She was so close. And I knew with every fiber within me, with my very essence, that I must reach her."

She was staring at him wide-eyed, almost in disbelief. And Jack wondered if perhaps he'd overestimated the old man's ability to be convincing. "And me? What did you think was happening to me while you were chasing this fantasy?"

There was hesitation, and Nathaniel's dark eyes narrowed ever so slightly at the question. "It is a regret, my dear. I did not do well by you. But I am happy to see you and Jack together now. He can help heal any wounds that have been inflicted on you by your past. If you allow it."

She gazed at Nathaniel with an unreadable expression, and Jack could suddenly feel a tumult of emotion within her getting ready to explode. "That does not explain now. What I'm seeing now. You seem so different to me, not so—"

"Ill?" Nathaniel said.

"Yes, I suppose."

"Nathaniel, in his pursuit of a connection with your mother, has relocated his primary consciousness," Jack said flatly.

"You said that before. What does it mean?" She said, looking at both her husband and father with almost accusation.

"It means, my dear, that my primary living, my most acute awareness, now exists in this dimension. This way, your mother and I are together and will be so until my transition."

"Transition?" she repeated breathlessly.

"My death, of course."

Chapter 30

What is Possible

Emma stared at her father incredulously and then returned her focus to her husband beside her. "His deterioration. It really isn't just physical."

"No," Jack said quietly. "It was the result of an active quest to achieve existence here, closer to your mother."

"My mother is a ghost?"

"No, Emma," Nathaniel replied sternly. "Not a ghost, a spirit who is able to fully actualize at times on this plane. It takes quite an investment of energy to be here. That is why I don't want you two here for long. I've chosen the consequences of being here. And Jack has graciously and selflessly chosen to be in charge of what is left of my corporeal self on your plane while it is there."

"Using me?" she murmured.

"No, Emma, you must accept that Jack connected with you long ago to help you. Can't you remember the man from Belle Coeur?" A brief flash of a young man with longish blonde hair in the corridors of the great house traveled across her mind.

And then, she stood up. This was so much, so much to take in. "I don't know. All of this is so difficult to believe, to accept. I want to see my mother. Is she here?"

"No," Jack was beside her. "Only Nathaniel can connect with her this way. He is existing on two planes at once."

"Two planes?" she whispered with disbelief.

"Your mother, she visits you often, Emma, speaks to you, sees you in dreams," her father said a bit frantically.

"I want to leave," she said, suddenly feeling everything inside her collapsing on itself, just shutting down. "This, all of this, it's too much."

And then Jack was beside her, his hand on her arm. "Emma, I dearly hoped this would help, help you understand."

And then Nathaniel added somberly, "I am so sorry, Emma. It is my deepest wish that you find happiness."

Her head had begun to pound, so much, so much to soak in. She knew in that instant that she had to get away, away from them. On an impulse, she pulled away from Jack, turning and then heading through the doorway.

She moved without looking back, rapidly down the hallway and through to the outside. She had to get some air to think clearly. In the semidarkness, she flew down the staircase without thought to the courtyard when a somewhat familiar and yet unyielding rush of dizziness overtook her.

⚜

Emmeline's eyes gradually opened in the morning light of the attic room. She'd been sent to bed with no supper, and her stomach panged her so.

Slowly, she sat up in the bed, her body aching slightly in discomfort. And immediately she saw that across the room was the young man — the same one from the long hall of portraits. He was just standing there, staring out the dormer window.

"Why are you here?" She murmured. She wasn't at all sure that she wasn't dreaming. As a result, she didn't question things like how he got in the house with no one seeing, or who he really was, because she didn't actually believe at that moment that he was real.

He didn't look at her, just continued to stare out that window. "Seems I've made a mess of things, Emma. I didn't intend to."

She pulled herself up to a sitting position in her bed. "How so?" She said, still terribly sleepy yet so very hungry.

Then he turned to her, and she had to admit he did look troubled. "I wasn't really trying to upset you or control you."

She frowned, wondering what on earth he could be babbling about. "Weren't you?" she replied a bit groggily, but then again, she was half-asleep.

Then a slight smile, "I didn't intend for you to be unhappy about it."

"Best of everything, usually impossible. And where are we now, young blonde man?" she said softly.

And then his eyes focused intently on her. "You've been traveling again."

❦

Once more, Emma opened her eyes. She sat up, frowning. Back to this once more, there was so much repetition. Evidently, she'd been reclining on the sofa in the parlor. And looking down, she noticed she was wearing the wine-colored evening dress. Her head throbbed dreadfully. This was really too much to deal with in such a short span of time. It was the dress, the one she'd worn the evening she and her father had gone to Dr. Fallon's house, Jack Fallon, now her husband. She glanced around the parlor with a bit of confusion because she'd expected, well, oddly expected to see Jack here or perhaps even Nathaniel. But there was neither. She, in fact, was entirely alone. As she brought her feet to the floor, there was an intense disorientation, so strong, a strange sort of fogginess in her mind. And then the footsteps behind her. She stood up and turned to the doorway, and again that keen dizziness passed through her, almost as though she would lose consciousness, but she was no longer alone now.

"Hold on. I know it's difficult." The voice was soft, feminine, familiar, and yet not. After all, when one speaks, they don't really hear their own voice as another might.

The woman glided into the center of the room. She wore blue, light blue, a color she had seen on her mother, but it wasn't her mother, though the resemblance was striking.

"This just can't be," she whispered from a throat still choked with shock and apprehension. Because this, all of this moment had a strangulated intangible quality to it. After all, how could she possibly be standing across from, well, herself.

"So many things can be possible, Emma. Maybe not all advisable, but indeed possible."

"I don't—why?"

"Am I here? Because you seemed like you needed a friend. And I heard somewhere once that a woman's best friend is herself."

"That sounds ridiculous," she mumbled.

The blonde woman, because she was having real problems accepting that this was indeed her, looked at her with an odd sort of understanding expression. But yes, of course, who would indeed understand her better than herself. "I'd forgotten how I was, how extraordinarily defensive."

"What are—" then she stopped herself. And started again, "Then how exactly old are you?"

"Thirty-one."

"Really?" She tried to take that in, around six years from now.

"And are you still living in this house?"

Her older self wore a shawl, sort of paisley, but mostly ecru-colored. The lady in blue moved to the bergere chair near the couch and sat down, smoothly arranging her skirts around her. That was something she would do, had done. Wardrobe etiquette had been relentlessly pressed on her at Aunt Adeleine's.

"Yes, she certainly did like to have things her way, didn't she?"

"Aunt Adeleine, you mean?" Then she understood, "You saw my thoughts."

"Feels a bit like my thoughts, Emma. You know this won't last long, this meeting. It's difficult, even more difficult than what you just experienced with Nathaniel. I won't answer questions about the future, not specifically, but there is something I'd like to talk about."

"Jack," she murmured. "Did he send you here?"

"Of course not. He'll be furious when he hears about this. He's very protective of me, you know."

She frowned a bit. That didn't sound terrible, having someone who was protective. "But you know what he did, I mean all the things he's done."

"Of course, he tricked you into marrying him, seduced you with his mesmerism."

Her throat went dry at the mention of the word seduced. "Yes, I didn't know what I was doing."

"Hmm," she murmured. "Well, I suppose you might say that. But I am here to tell you a bit about Jack."

"You want me to stay with him."

"I want you to understand him better. Everything you see is colored by your past experiences. You're very emotional right now. Things do get better inside of you, I mean, much calmer. But if you were in a calmer state right now, you might look at everything differently." She sighed with frustration, overwhelmed by a maelstrom of emotions coming from all about her, from this woman, herself. She could feel so much. "Try to separate things, Emma. I know it's difficult."

She stood up, walking across the parlor. "How could he trick me? And Nathaniel, how could he be so selfish? Leaving me at Belle Coeur when it was such, such a terrible place."

"Well, I can't speak for Nathaniel. We all make our choices. But as for Jack deceiving you, well, of course, he shouldn't have, but he did feel desperate. He does care for Nathaniel greatly, feels obligated to him, and you, well, he'd waited so long for you."

She turned around, staring at her older self with confusion. "Waited?"

"Yes, of course, the visions, the young man at Belle Coeur. He made contact with you long ago, was so worried about you, truly only wanted your safety and happiness."

"And I would only be happy if I married him?"

"You certainly could be if you wanted. He's a lovely husband, attentive, passionate, protective, and a challenge at times. But if you aren't challenged, how do you grow?"

She stared at her other self with a hint of sadness. She was painting such an enticing picture. "I have to be able to trust him."

"Yes, of course, then give him time to win that trust. Give him time, Emma, give both of you time. It's a life worth cultivating."

The dizziness swirled. "I don't know."

She smiled again. "Consider it. I have to go now. Jack's looking for me. Be happy, my dear. I've learned happiness doesn't just come. You must seek it out and hold onto it with a steady grip."

She paused for a moment, reflecting, staring back at her older, more serene self. And then she closed her eyes and felt everything swirl strangely about her. Now, there were arms around her, strong arms holding her up. The cool rush of the night air surrounded her as she opened her eyes. They were standing on the outside staircase, and she was leaning against Jack, who held her tightly. "Emma," he whispered with concern in his voice. "Are you all right?"

He held her against him, and she remembered the comfort of just being next to him. She looked around with surprise. "It's nighttime."

"Yes, that happens sometimes. Traveling isn't precise, and time is a funny thing."

She turned, pulling away from him and descending to the courtyard. Then she stopped, turning and staring at him intently. "I want to trust you, Jack. I need—" She paused, still feeling the dizzying effects of the traveling. The night air helped snap her back into awareness. She needed to think, just a few moments, to clear her mind.

"Emma, listen to me," he said, standing before her, hands on her shoulders, but again she pulled away, walking more deeply into the courtyard and sitting in one of the cast-iron chairs.

She looked up, and he was standing on the other side of the table, watching her with such concern. He was afraid. She could feel it, truly afraid he'd lost her. "This isn't simple for me, Jack."

How very vulnerable he seemed to her in this moment, a bit like that young man in her vision staring out the window of her attic room. "I'm sorry. I should have given things more time, you more time I—" Then he stopped. It was going to be more explanations that she'd heard.

"I can't be controlled, Jack, manipulated. I've spent so long living a life that was at other people's whims, convenience. I can't worry if—"

"If you can trust me?"

His hands were on the back of the chair on the other side of the table. He nodded emphatically, "Of course, but the truth is I need you, Emma. I truly need you with me, and if you give me time, I will gain your trust, your love."

She looked at him oddly. It struck her at that moment that this was indeed such a strange thing to say because she did love him. That was what made this so difficult. She was completely in love with him. She wasn't sure when it began, but here it was, enmeshed in her, wrapped around her so completely. But she couldn't let that make her weak. "There can't be any more secrets, you know, Jack. I need to know and understand always what is going on."

She saw a slight smile fleetingly come to his lips. He knew it, of course — knew that now she was negotiating terms. "Yes, that would please me greatly, my love, to have a true partner in all things."

She nodded. She knew it was clear now to both of them what she would do. She would stay and "cultivate" things as her older self had advised.

She stood up and walked over to him, facing him with strength. "All right, Jack, I will stay with you and be your wife."

At this, he pulled her gently into his arms, and she felt real peace as he whispered to her. "I love you, Emma."

She would say it back to him in time. Because she did love him, truly, though she was pragmatic, and believing that life with Jack Fallon would ever be simple was something she simply could not do.

Finis

The Story of Enid
Vol. 2 of The Clandestine Exploits of a Werewolf
6 x 9 Softcover 254 pages
ISBN 978-1-61342-453-7

What happens when your one true love reincarnates, and you just happen to be a werewolf?

Ethan Garraint is an old soul. He has been alive for hundreds of years, battling countless challenges and foes along the way—not the least of which was living through the genocide of the Cathar people at Montsegur, a society that wholly embraced him despite his lycanthropic nature. But in Volume 2 of The Clandestine Exploits of a Werewolf, he faces a dilemma that brings his past and present full circle, merging them both.

The Broken Vow
Vol. 1 of The Clandestine Exploits of a Werewolf
6 x 9 Softcover & Hardcover 204 pages
ISBN 978-1-61342-133-8
ISBN (Hardcover) 978-1-61342-420-9

In the heart of every man, there is a history. In the heart of every monster, there is a story. In this first installment of The Clandestine Exploits of a Werewolf, Ethan Garraint is on a vendetta that begins in the heart of the Pyrenees with the fall of Montségur and leads him to the streets of New Orleans nearly five hundred years later. But the person he chases isn't really a man anymore, and Ethan has been a werewolf for almost a millennium. With the aid of a gifted seer, he is on a blood hunt that will culminate in a journey that crosses the line between heaven and earth and ends somewhere in between.

The Lady in the Blue Dress
6 x 9 Softcover & Hardcover 214 pages
ISBN 978-1-61342-600-5
ISBN (Hardcover) 978-1-61342-418-6

When she was a child, Mika Devalieur was introduced to her grandmother's most precious possession — a priceless and mysterious painting that she simply called The Lady in the Blue Dress. Upon Adele St. Clair's death, the painting is left in the care of her granddaughter with only one stipulation. Mika must hand over the family heirloom to a total stranger. Mika Devalieur desperately wants to deny her beloved grandmother's last request, but she can't. Torn between her Gran's last wishes and her desire to hold onto the Lady, she ultimately journeys to rural Virginia, where an enigmatic man shows her that this painting is only the beginning.

What quickly becomes clear is that James Clairmont knows much more about her and the Lady than he is letting on. He begins to slowly unravel a powerful supernatural connection that spans three generations of her family. Mika finds herself desperate to uncover the entire truth before she falls in love with a man filled with so many secrets — secrets about him, about her, and most especially about The Lady in the Blue Dress. (First published on Kindle Vella, episodes 1-23.)

Dumaine Street
6 x 9 Softcover & Hardcover 306 pages
ISBN 978-1-61342-902-0
ISBN (Hardcover) 978-1-61342-416-2

Voices in her head, catastrophic emotions, hallucinations — Rebecca Wells is more than convinced that she is losing her mind. And as a last-ditch effort, she contacts a self-professed counselor who seems convinced he can help.

Gabriel Sutton has abandoned the world of medicine to navigate a realm filled with psychic phenomena. Diagnosing Becca with extreme empathic abilities, he struggles to help her stabilize her gifts while trying desperately not to fall in love with his patient.

From the realm of vulnerability into a crusade to use their profound gifts to rescue others from peril on the other side of death, these two follow an astonishing and unpredictable path into each other's hearts.

The Tethering
A Portent of Crows
6 x 9 Softcover & Hardcover 201 pages
ISBN 978-1-61342-599-2
ISBN (Hardcover) 978-1-61342-419-3

Deborah Brandt's beloved Aunt Gena always told her that she was special, a bit different, and would have to live her life, unlike other people. Of course, this she disregarded as the ramblings of her lovely but notably eccentric aunt. Although there were the things that Aunt Gena said that seemed true — like Deborah being sensitive to energy shifts, having potentially psychic impressions, and dreaming of a spirit guide — none of it could be real. But the most ridiculous thing that her Aunt Gena told her before she died was that someone special was out there for her. She said that he was an extraordinary man who was not only her perfect match but someone who she would learn from so that they could help the world in difficult times. How ridiculous! It sounds like a fairy tale, and no such person exists.

Daniel Wren is unique. He has been raised and trained from a young age to hone his psychic gifts. He lives in a world unimagined by most. And he has been waiting for years to contact his counterpart, soulmate, if you will. But the problem is that she is painfully unaware of the type of life that he lives and the life she would be entering into if they came together.

His dilemma becomes how best to proceed. How can he win her over and move forward before outside forces take that decision away from him?

Travels into the Breach
Accounts of a Reluctant Mystic
6 x 9 Softcover & Hardcover 171 pages
ISBN 978-1-61342-323-3
ISBN (Hardcover) 978-1-61342-417-9

At first glance, his life seems quiet, serene, and even un-eventful. Malachi McKellan, a 65-year-old widower and author of esoteric books, lives largely as a recluse in a house situated just off the banks of Bayou St. John in New Orleans. But unbeknownst to most, he is also a bit of a detective, a specific kind of detective whose specialty is psychic attacks. Alongside his lifelong companion and spirit guide Simon Tull, a 19th-century, 20-something English gent, Malachi battles the unseen, and is an unacknowledged hero to the most vulnerable. Most of the population have no idea what is really happening beneath the surface of the world in which they live.

In this collection of adventures, Malachi McKellan and Simon Tull wage war against the most insidious elements of the paranormal. In *The Three*, Malachi and Simon come to the aid of a young woman being victimized by a group of dark witches. An old apartment building is the scene of an unimaginable battle against monstrous forces in *The Lost Soul*. Malachi and Simon find themselves strategizing against a psychic vampire in *Obsession*, and *The Hotel* turns back time to the 1980s where Malachi confronts a demonic spirit. In *Between*, a past life is revisited as Malachi attempts to rescue a beloved sister from committing her existence to vengeance, and *The Wedding* takes a personal turn when Malachi must confront painful truths while endeavoring to protect his niece from a potentially devastating union.

Travel into the breach with a pair of paranormal warriors who choose to confront overwhelming forces on a battlefield unsuspected by most.

Gravier's Bookshop
A New Orleans Paranormal Mystery (#1)
6 x 9 Softcover & Hardcover 172 pages
ISBN 978-1-61342-288-5
ISBN (Hardcover) 978-1-61342-411-7

Max Gravier had no intention of becoming a recluse, but after his wife's death it seems his life is heading in that direction. He spends his time running Gravier's Bookshop on Magazine Street and occasionally on the quiet helps the police solve a crime with his psychic sensitivities. That is until he answers Caroline Breslin's call, a cry for help out of his dreams that draws him into a fierce battle for a young woman's soul.

In this first installment of The New Orleans Paranormal Mystery series, Caroline Breslin, an amazingly gifted empath, is determined to strike out on her own and has moved out from the protection of her family home. All is going extremely well until, of course, she comes under siege from a devastating supernatural attack. The last thing Caroline wants is to run back to her family for help, even though she is painfully in over her head. What she really needs is a knight in shining armor — or maybe just that guy that keeps haunting her dreams.

Join them and the whole Breslin family psychic clan in this first installment of The New Orleans Paranormal Mystery Series where you'll travel into a new world just a few steps into the turbulent realm of the unseen.

The Hotel Mandolin
A New Orleans Paranormal Mystery (#2)
6 x 9 Softcover & Hardcover 146 pages
ISBN 978-1-61342-290-8
ISBN (Hardcover) 978-1-61342-412-4

Peril is wrapped up in the most enticing of disguises in *The Hotel Mandolin*, the second installment of The New Orleans Paranormal Mystery series. It's opulent, classic, and one of the most renowned hotels nestled deep in New Orleans' famous business district, but something is amiss at The Hotel Mandolin.

PI Peter Norfleet is calling out the big guns to help him investigate a recent suicide at the famous establishment — his good friend Max Gravier, a formidable psychic, and his girlfriend, Caroline Breslin, a talented empath. But none of them can seem to scratch the surface of this puzzle, no one except Cassie Breslin, Caroline's clairvoyant mother, who has somehow tapped into an unexpected connection with a tragic ghost from the turn of the century. And the more she uncovers, the more dangerous and malevolent the mystery becomes

The House at Pritchard Place
A New Orleans Paranormal Mystery (#3)
6 x 9 Softcover & Hardcover 138 pages
ISBN 978-1-61342-292-2
ISBN (Hardcover) 978-1-61342-413-1

Nothing is really wrong with the old Warrick House on Dante St. except that there most certainly is. Nothing is exactly wrong with its new mysterious owner except that Elise is sure that something doesn't add up. It isn't obvious, but sometimes the most dangerous things aren't.

In the third installment of The New Orleans Paranormal Mystery series, with the help of her very psychic sister and her children, the Breslin clan, Elise Ashford is about to embark on a wild rescue mission straight into another dimension that will land her squarely somewhere she doesn't expect, right back into her past. She'll land full circle; in a childhood home whose memory still haunts her to this day -- *The House at Pritchard Place.*

Treading on Borrowed Time
6 x 9 Softcover & Hardcover 223 pages
ISBN 978-1-61342-214-4
ISBN (Hardcover) 978-1-61342-436-0

For Julia Moreau, life seems complicated. Emerging from a failed marriage and managing a lifetime of diabetes, she lives alone in her childhood home where she communicates with the spirit of her Great Aunt Lilia. But Julia doesn't have a clue what complicated is until she is thrust into being the key chess piece in a match between two powerful men of extraordinary abilities on the wild hunt for a mystical creature hidden in the heart of New Orleans' French Quarter. Will Julia lose her soul to the karma of a devastating past life or her heart to the love of a man driven by dark forces? What is clear is that whichever way she turns she is *Treading on Borrowed Time.*

Sanctuary of Echoes
6 x 9 Softcover & Hardcover 371 pages
ISBN 978-1-61342-211-3
ISBN (Hardcover) 978-1-61342-409-4

Ghosts unacknowledged do not sleep.

Corey Knight has resigned herself to a quiet, reclusive life spent living out the rest of her days in her childhood home on the fringes of New Orleans' French Quarter. But the unexpected specter of her deceased father plunges her into a mad quest for a missing supernatural weapon unearthed long ago. And unfortunately, her only ally is a lost love she once betrayed.

Iain Shaw returns to New Orleans, a city he abandoned a decade before while fleeing a devastating past. Here, he is forced to confront it again in the visage of the woman he once adored - one that he is now determined to get back at any cost.

Follow them both in a wild paranormal tale of discovery and redemption as they confront and unearth the echoes of a buried and unyielding truth that once tore them irreparably apart.

A Quiet Moment
6 x 9 Softcover & Hardcover 273 pages
ISBN 978-1-61342-326-4
ISBN (Hardcover) 978-1-61342-435-3

Jacob Wyss is caught in a rut, in fact on the verge of being engulfed by it. After an excruciating and disillusioning divorce, his life as an artist in a sleepy-college town at the foot of the Appalachian Mountains has become quiet, routine, and maddening in its predictability. One wintry day, his deep restlessness drives him out in precarious conditions to a largely empty bookstore nearly devoid of another living soul, nearly.

Aimee Marston isn't like everyone else. On the surface, she lives a sedate life working as a feature writer for a small local newspaper in addition to several other editorial jobs to help make ends meet. But just beneath, her existence is largely not her own. She is a sensitive, an empathetic psychic, guided by her calling to use her gifts to help others. Unfortunately, as a result, her secretiveness has made her defensive, protective of herself, and prevented her from having much of a life.

A psychic call for help sends Aimee out on a freezing January morning where her destiny and Jacob's collide sending both their lives spiraling onto an unexpected and often disturbing track. Two lonely souls connect, not by accident, but by design. Theirs is the intersection of two spiritual paths, two lovers who must struggle to overcome the phantoms of a past life, as well as the challenges of their own inner demons to carve out an extraordinary future together.

A Ghost of a Chance
6 x 9 Softcover & Hardcover 230 pages
ISBN 978-1-61342-162-8
ISBN (Hardcover) 978-1-61342-440-7

You never know what's coming next.

Jack Brennan, an ambitious high-powered attorney, dies. But that's not the end, rather only the beginning. He finds himself constrained to an inexplicable afterlife as an earth-bound spirit trapped in an old Virginia farmhouse. His only companion is a very much living, reclusive writer of campy vampire novels. The maddening problem is that Hallie does not know he is there, nor that he is somewhat reluctantly falling in love with her.

Hallie Barkly is recovering from a painful and disillusioning divorce. Out of the ashes of her former life, she has managed to somehow forge a career and exorcise her demons by writing under the pseudonym of Sebastian Winters. Slowly, she is awakening to the fact that she is not alone.

Their lives intersect, and two unconventional lovers are brought together under insurmountable circumstances. Together they must battle an unseen force hell-bent on possessing Hallie's life and bridge death itself to make possible what cannot be — to find a chance.

Dragonflies - Journeys into the Paranormal
6 x 9 Softcover & Hardcover 176 pages
ISBN 978-1-88756-072-6
ISBN (Hardcover) 979-8-32548-418-6

In every form of creation, there is a blueprint for living, for experience, for interpretation. In flight, they can twist, turn, alter direction, pause in midair, and even fly backward. The dragonfly is the master of adaptability. They are a living prism, refracting light, and color, seemingly shifting their essence.

The lesson the dragonfly gives is that life is never what it appears to be.

In "The Wizard," as a novice practitioner of magic, Aurora Finn finds herself battling against the illusions of a powerful wizard intent on separating her from the world she knows. "The Sojourners" is a gentle story of a mother and daughter whose tenancy in an old Virginia farmhouse uncovers the trials and sorrows of its former occupants. A bookstore clerk gets an extraordinary customer on Halloween night in "Late One Night at Berstrums Books." In "The Tear," a woman coping with her fatal illness unknowingly begins a track on a mystical journey that will entirely restructure her vision of the world.

These stories follow the path of the dragonfly imbued with the momentum and energy of change, taking a winding and treacherous journey that ultimately leads to truth buried beneath perception.

Breaking Through the Pale
6 x 9 Softcover 134 pages
ISBN 978-1-88756-045-0

Journey with metaphysical author Evelyn Klebert into a collection of short stories that travel beyond the pale into the unpredictable realm of the paranormal.

In "A Grey Mourning," a disillusioned man encounters a mysterious being on the foggy streets of New Orleans. "Contact" is a tale of automatic writing, when a young artist establishes communication with a spirit guide, and the victim of a car crash unravels the true nature of her existence in "Dancing on the Threshold." The final tale is called "Isolation," in which a confused and disoriented woman finds herself in an old, quaint house where she must piece together the mystical implications surrounding her predicament.

The Witches' Own
6 x 9 Softcover & Hardcover 140 pages
ISBN 978-1-61342-058-4
ISBN (Hardcover) 978-1-61342-428-5

On the surface things seem quiet and serene in the picturesque coastal village of Kilmarnock, Virginia. But something unseen roams its lush forests as the past and present collide and the unthinkable begins to wreak its vengeance. Young Lucy Bonner is executed for witchcraft in the town's distant and brutal past. Her death triggers an unholy chain of events which grasp at the restless heart of novelist Peter McQuade, spurring him towards a quest to uncover the dark and terrifying truth.

The Left Palm
And Other Halloween Tales of the Supernatural
6 x 9 Softcover & Hardcover 122 pages
ISBN 978-1-93493-556-9
ISBN (Hardcover) 978-1-61342-442-1

Halloween is the time of year when that veil between worlds is thinned, and you can just catch a quick glimpse into the realm of the unknowable. In this collection of short stories, Evelyn Klebert takes you to a place where ordinary life splinters into the sphere of the paranormal.

The journey begins with one woman's unstoppable quest for vengeance against a supernatural creature in "Wolves" and continues in an old historical graveyard where a horrifying discovery is uncovered in "Emma Fallon." In "The Soul Shredder," a psychiatrist's unusual patient opens his eyes to a disturbing new view of reality, while in "Wildflowers," a woman strikes up a supernatural friendship with impossible implications. And in "The Left Palm," a fortuneteller in the French Quarter receives a most unexpected and terrifying customer.

White Harbor Road
And Other Tales of Paranormal Romance
6 x 9 Softcover & Hardcover 152 pages
ISBN 978-1-61342-066-9
ISBN (Hardcover) 978-1-61342-441-4

A psychic soul mate, a time traveler, a horror writer, and an enigmatic stranger take a selection of resilient, life-battered heroines to a place of paranormal healing and transformation. In this collection of short stories, *White Harbor Road* is the last stop where life's burdens and hardships evolve into something unexpected.

Explanations
6 x 9 Softcover 82 pages
ISBN 978-1-93493-515-6

In this, her second poetry collection, Evelyn Klebert takes us down the intricate path of a personal journey. Life with its particular struggles, pitfalls, and ultimately triumphs clearly begins to mirror a universal path, the quest for answers that we all ultimately pursue. In this reflective, esoteric collection we can all explore and seek some of life's elemental mysteries and hopefully when all is said and done emerge with some *Explanations*.

Considerations
6 x 9 Softcover 84 pages
ISBN 978-1-88756-062-7

Sometimes the struggle to understand the meaning and complexities of living comes down to a single moment of introspection or a fleeting yet meaningful reflection. This collection of poetry by Evelyn Klebert takes you down a winding path of self-discovery where the resolution may not always be absolute, but the journey is indeed unforgettable. It a wide and varied map of inspired poetry for your examination and consideration.

Appointment with the Unknown
The Hotel Stories
6 x 9 Softcover & Hardcover 155 pages
ISBN 978-1-61342-360-8
ISBN (Hardcover) 978-1-61342-421-6

A hotel, for most, represents a normal place, a predictable realm of commonality. One might even go as far to say a safe space, the reliable where nothing particularly unusual is expected to happen. Or is it? Dimensional traveling, spirit guides, mystical storms, and soul mates separated by time are only a few elements dotting this supernatural landscape. Drop into a collection of romantic paranormal stories where that place of commonality is only the threshold, the jumping-off point, for extraordinary adventures into the unknown.

Visit Evelyn's website at:
www.evelynklebert.com
Cornerstone Book Publishers
www.cornerstonepublishers.com